ZEBRA
and
Other
Stories

CHAIM POTOK

ZEBRA and Other Stories

Alfred A. Knopf
New York

THIS IS A BORZOI BOOK PUBLISHED BY ALFRED A. KNOPF, INC.

Published in the United States of America by Alfred A. Knopf, Inc., New York,
and simultaneously in Canada by Random House of Canada Limited, Toronto.
Distributed by Random House, Inc., New York.

Five of these stories have been previously published, some in slightly different form: "Zebra" in *The Philadelphia Inquirer Sunday Magazine*; "B.B." in *The American Voice*; "Moon" in *Image*; "Isabel" in *The Kenyon Review*; and "Max" in *The New England Review*.

www.randomhouse.com/kids/

Library of Congress Cataloging-in-Publication Data

Potok, Chaim

Zebra and Other Stories / by Chaim Potok. — 1st ed.

p. cm.

Contents: Zebra — B.B. — Moon — Nava — Isabel — Max.

Summary: A collection of stories about six different young people who each experience a life-changing event.

1. Short stories, American. [1. Short stories.] I. Title.

PZ7. P8399Ze 1998
[Fic] — dc21 98-4769

ISBN 0-679-85440-1 (trade)
ISBN 0-679-95440-6 (lib. bdg.)

Printed in the United States of America
10 9 8 7 6 5 4 3 2 1
First Edition

To

DON SANDNER

listener and healer

Acknowledgments

Many people were of considerable help to me in the writing of these stories: Barbara and Robert Holmes, William Holmes, Paige and Bernard Kaplan, Sheldon Levin, Akiva Potok, James Stovall. To all of them, my deepest thanks.

C.P.

Contents

ZEBRA
and
Other
Stories

Zebra

His name was Adam Martin Zebrin, but everyone in his neighborhood knew him as Zebra.

He couldn't remember when he began to be called by that name. Perhaps they started to call him Zebra when he first began running. Or maybe he began running when they started to call him Zebra.

He loved the name and he loved to run.

When he was very young, his parents took him to a zoo, where he saw zebras for the first time. They were odd-looking creatures, like stubby horses, short-legged, thick-necked, with dark and white stripes.

Then one day he went with his parents to a movie about Africa, and he saw zebras, hundreds of them, thundering across a grassy plain, dust rising in boiling brown clouds.

Was he already running before he saw that movie, or did he begin to run afterward? No one seemed able to remember.

He would go running through the neighborhood for the sheer joy of feeling the wind on his face. People said that when he ran he arched his head up and back, and his face kind of flattened out. One of his teachers told him it was clever to run that way, his balance was better. But the truth was he ran that way, his head thrown back, because he loved to feel the wind rushing across his neck.

Each time, after only a few minutes of running, his legs would begin to feel wondrously light. He would run past the school and the homes on the street beyond the church. All the neighbors knew him and would wave and call out, "Go, Zebra!" And sometimes one or two of their dogs would run with him awhile, barking.

He would imagine himself a zebra on the African plain. Running.

There was a hill on Franklin Avenue, a steep hill. By the time he reached that hill, he would feel his legs so light it was as if he had no legs at all and was flying. He would begin to descend the hill, certain as he ran that he needed only to give himself the slightest push and off he would go, and instead of a zebra he would become the bird he had once seen in a movie about Alaska, he would swiftly change into an eagle, soaring higher and higher, as light as the gentlest breeze, the cool wind caressing his arms and legs and neck.

Then, a year ago, racing down Franklin Avenue, he had given himself that push and had begun to turn into an eagle, when a huge rushing shadow appeared in his line of vision and crashed into him and plunged him into a darkness from which he emerged very, very slowly....

"Never, never, *never* run down that hill so fast that you can't stop at the corner," his mother had warned him again and again.

His schoolmates and friends kept calling him Zebra even

after they all knew that the doctors had told him he would never be able to run like that again.

His leg would heal in time, the doctors said, and perhaps in a year or so the brace would come off. But they were not at all certain about his hand. From time to time his injured hand, which he still wore in a sling, would begin to hurt. The doctors said they could find no cause for the pain.

One morning, during Mr. Morgan's geography class, Zebra's hand began to hurt badly. He sat staring out the window at the sky. Mr. Morgan, a stiff-mannered person in his early fifties, given to smart suits and dapper bow ties, called on him to respond to a question. Zebra stumbled about in vain for the answer. Mr. Morgan told him to pay attention to the geography *inside* the classroom and not to the geography outside.

"In this class, young man, you will concentrate your attention upon the earth, not upon the sky," Mr. Morgan said.

Later, in the schoolyard during the midmorning recess, Zebra stood near the tall fence, looking out at the street and listening to the noises behind him.

His schoolmates were racing about, playing exuberantly, shouting and laughing with full voices. Their joyous sounds went ringing through the quiet street.

Most times Zebra would stand alongside the basketball court or behind the wire screen at home plate and watch the games. That day, because his hand hurt so badly, he stood alone behind the chain-link fence of the schoolyard.

That's how he happened to see the man. And that's how the man happened to see him.

One minute the side street on which the school stood was strangely empty, without people or traffic, without even any of the dogs that often roamed about the neighborhood—vacant and silent, as if it were already in the full heat of summer. The red-brick ranch house that belonged to Mr. Morgan, and the white clapboard two-story house in which Mrs. English lived, and the other homes on the street, with their columned front porches and their back patios, and the tall oaks—all stood curiously still in the warm golden light of the mid-morning sun.

Then a man emerged from wide and busy Franklin Avenue at the far end of the street.

Zebra saw the man stop at the corner and stand looking at a public trash can. He watched as the man poked his hand into the can and fished about but seemed to find nothing he wanted. He withdrew the hand and, raising it to shield his eyes from the sunlight, glanced at the street sign on the lamppost.

He started to walk up the street in the direction of the school.

He was tall and wiry, and looked to be about forty years old. In his right hand he carried a bulging brown plastic bag. He wore a khaki army jacket, a blue denim shirt, blue jeans, and brown cowboy boots. His gaunt face and muscular neck were reddened by exposure to the sun. Long brown hair spilled out below his dark-blue farmer's cap. On the front of the cap, in large orange letters, were the words LAND ROVER.

He walked with his eyes on the sidewalk and the curb, as if looking for something, and he went right past Zebra without noticing him.

Zebra's hand hurt very much. He was about to turn away when he saw the man stop and look around and peer up at the red-brick wall of the school. The man set down the bag and took off his cap and stuffed it into a pocket of his jacket. From one of his jeans pockets he removed a handkerchief, with which he then wiped his face. He shoved the handkerchief back into the pocket and put the cap back on his head.

Then he turned and saw Zebra.

He picked up the bag and started down the street to where Zebra was standing. When the man was about ten feet away, Zebra noticed that the left sleeve of his jacket was empty.

The man came up to Zebra and said in a low, friendly, shy voice, "Hello."

Zebra answered with a cautious "Hello," trying not to look at the empty sleeve, which had been tucked into the man's jacket pocket.

The man asked, with a distinct Southern accent, "What's your name, son?"

Zebra said, "Adam."

"What kind of school is this here school, Adam?"

"It's a good school," Zebra answered.

"How long before you-all begin your summer vacation?"

"Three days," Zebra said.

"Anything special happen here during the summer?"

"During the summer? Nothing goes on here. There are no classes."

"What do you-all do during the summer?"

"Some of us go to camp. Some of us hang around. We find things to do."

Zebra's hand had begun to tingle and throb. Why was the man asking all those questions? Zebra thought maybe he shouldn't be talking to him at all. He seemed vaguely menacing in that army jacket, the dark-blue cap with the words LAND

ROVER on it in orange letters, and the empty sleeve. Yet there was kindness in his gray eyes and ruddy features.

The man gazed past Zebra at the students playing in the yard. "Adam, do you think your school would be interested in having someone teach an art class during the summer?"

That took Zebra by surprise. "An *art* class?"

"Drawing, sculpting, things like that."

Zebra was trying *very hard* not to look at the man's empty sleeve. "I don't know. . . ."

"Where's the school office, Adam?"

"On Washington Avenue. Go to the end of the street and turn right."

"Thanks," the man said. He hesitated a moment. Then he asked, in a quiet voice, "What happened to you, Adam?"

"A car hit me," Zebra said. "It was my fault."

The man seemed to wince.

For a flash of a second, Zebra thought to ask the man what had happened to *him*. The words were on his tongue. But he kept himself from saying anything.

The man started back up the street, carrying the brown plastic bag.

Zebra suddenly called, "Hey, mister."

The man stopped and turned. "My name is John Wilson," he said softly.

"Mr. Wilson, when you go into the school office, you'll see signs on two doors. One says 'Dr. Winter,' and the other says 'Mrs. English.' Ask for Mrs. English."

Dr. Winter, the principal, was a disciplinarian and a grump. Mrs. English, the assistant principal, was generous and kind. Dr. Winter would probably tell the man to call his secretary for an appointment. Mrs. English might invite him into her office and offer him a cup of coffee and listen to what he had to say.

The man hesitated, looking at Zebra.

"Appreciate the advice," he said.

Zebra watched him walk to the corner.

Under the lamppost was a trash can. Zebra saw the man set down the plastic bag and stick his hand into the can and haul out a battered umbrella.

The man tried to open the umbrella, but its metal ribs were broken. The black fabric dangled flat and limp from the pole. He put the umbrella into the plastic bag and headed for the entrance to the school.

A moment later, Zebra heard the whistle that signaled the end of recess. He followed his classmates at a distance, careful to avoid anyone's bumping against his hand.

He sat through his algebra class, copying the problems on the blackboard while holding down his notebook with his left elbow. The sling chafed his neck and felt warm and clumsy on his bare arm. There were sharp pains now in the two curled fingers of his hand.

Right after the class he went downstairs to the office of Mrs. Walsh, a cheerful, gray-haired woman in a white nurse's uniform.

She said, "I'm sorry I can't do very much for you, Adam, except give you two Tylenols."

He swallowed the Tylenols down with water.

On his way back up to the second floor, he saw the man with the dark-blue cap emerge from the school office with Mrs. English. He stopped on the stairs and watched as the man and

Mrs. English stood talking together. Mrs. English nodded and smiled and shook the man's hand.

The man walked down the corridor, carrying the plastic bag, and left the school building.

Zebra went slowly to his next class.

The class was taught by Mrs. English, who came hurrying into the room some minutes after the bell had rung.

"I apologize for being late," she said, sounding a little out of breath. "There was an important matter I had to attend to."

Mrs. English was a tall, gracious woman in her forties. It was common knowledge that early in her life she had been a journalist on a Chicago newspaper and had written short stories, which she could not get published. Soon after her marriage to a doctor, she had become a teacher.

This was the only class Mrs. English taught.

Ten students from the upper school—seventh and eighth grades—were chosen every year for this class. They met for an hour three times a week and told one another stories. Each story would be discussed and analyzed by Mrs. English and the class.

Mrs. English called it a class in the *imagination*.

Zebra was grateful he did not have to take notes in this class. He had only to listen to the stories.

That day, Andrea, the freckle-faced, redheaded girl with very thick glasses who sat next to Zebra, told about a woman scientist who discovered a method of healing trees that had been blasted apart by lightning.

Mark, who had something wrong with his upper lip, told in his quavery voice about a selfish space cadet who stepped into a time machine and met his future self, who turned out to be a hateful person, and how the cadet then returned to the present and changed himself.

Kevin talked in blurred, high-pitched tones and often related parts of his stories with his hands. Mrs. English would quietly repeat many of his sentences. Today he told about an explorer who set out on a journey through a valley filled with yellow stones and surrounded by red mountains, where he encountered an army of green shadows that had been at war for hundreds of years with an army of purple shadows. The explorer showed them how to make peace.

When it was Zebra's turn, he told a story about a bird that one day crashed against a closed windowpane and broke a wing. A boy tried to heal the wing but couldn't. The bird died, and the boy buried it under a tree on his lawn.

When he had finished, there was silence. Everyone in the class was looking at him.

"You always tell such sad stories," Andrea said.

The bell rang. Mrs. English dismissed the class.

In the hallway, Andrea said to Zebra, "You know, you are a very gloomy life form."

"Andrea, get off my case," Zebra said.

He went out to the schoolyard for the midafternoon recess. On the other side of the chain-link fence was the man in the dark-blue cap.

Zebra went over to him.

"Hello again, Adam," the man said. "I've been waiting for you."

"Hello," said Zebra.

"Thanks much for suggesting I talk to Mrs. English."

"You're welcome."

"Adam, you at all interested in art?"

"No."

"You ever try your hand at it?"

"I've made drawings for class. I don't like it."

"Well, just in case you change your mind, I'm giving an art class in your school during the summer."

"I'm going to camp in August," Zebra said.

"There's the big long month of July."

"I don't think so," Zebra said.

"Well, okay, suit yourself. I'd like to give you something, a little thank-you gift."

He reached into an inside pocket and drew out a small pad and a pen. He placed the pad against the fence.

"Adam, you want to help me out a little bit here? Put your fingers through the fence and grab hold of the pad."

Extending the fingers of his right hand, Zebra held the pad to the fence and watched as the man began to work with the pen. He felt the pad move slightly.

"I need you to hold it real still," the man said.

He was standing bent over, very close to Zebra. The words LAND ROVER on his cap shone in the afternoon sunlight. As he worked, he glanced often at Zebra. His tongue kept pushing up against the insides of his cheeks, making tiny hills rise and fall on his face. Wrinkles formed intricate spidery webs in the skin below his gray eyes. On his smooth forehead, in the blue and purple shadows beneath the peak of his cap, lay glistening beads of sweat. And his hand—how dirty it was, the fingers and palm smudged with black ink and encrusted with colors.

Then Zebra glanced down and noticed the plastic bag near

the man's feet. It lay partly open. Zebra was able to see a large pink armless doll, a dull metallic object that looked like a dented frying pan, old newspapers, strings of cord, crumpled pieces of red and blue cloth, and the broken umbrella.

"One more minute is all I need," the man said.

He stepped back, looked at the pad, and nodded slowly. He put the pen back into his pocket and tore the top page from the pad. He rolled up the page and pushed it through the fence. Then he took the pad from Zebra.

"See you around, Adam," the man said, picking up the plastic bag.

Zebra unrolled the sheet of paper and saw a line drawing, a perfect image of his face.

He was looking at himself as if in a mirror. His long straight nose and thin lips and sad eyes and gaunt face; his dark hair and smallish ears and the scar on his forehead where he had hurt himself years before while roller skating.

In the lower right-hand corner of the page the man had written: "To ADAM, with thanks. John Wilson."

Zebra raised his eyes from the drawing. The man was walking away.

Zebra called out, "Mr. Wilson, all my friends call me Zebra."

The man turned, looking surprised.

"From my last name," Adam said. "Zebrin. Adam Martin Zebrin. They call me Zebra."

"Is that right?" the man said, starting back toward the fence. "Well, in that case you want to give me back that piece of paper."

He took the pad and pen from his pocket, placed the page

on the pad, and, with Zebra holding the pad to the fence, did something to the page and then handed it back.

"You take real good care of yourself, Zebra," the man said.

He went off toward Franklin Avenue.

Zebra looked at the drawing. The man had crossed out ADAM and over it had drawn an animal with a stubby neck and short legs and a striped body.

A zebra!

Its legs were in full gallop. It seemed as if it would gallop right off the page.

A strong breeze rippled across the drawing, causing it to flutter like a flag in Zebra's hand. He looked out at the street.

The man was walking slowly in the shadows of the tall oaks. Zebra had the odd sensation that all the houses on the street had turned toward the man and were watching him as he walked along. How strange that was: the windows and porches and columns and front doors following intently the slow walk of that tall, one-armed man—until he turned into Franklin Avenue and was gone.

The whistle blew, and Zebra went inside. Seated at his desk, he slipped the drawing carefully into one of his notebooks.

From time to time he glanced at it.

Just before the bell signaled the end of the school day, he looked at it again.

Now *that* was strange!

He thought he remembered that the zebra had been drawn directly over his name: the head over the A and the tail over the M. Didn't it seem now to have moved a little beyond the A?

Probably he was running a fever again. He would run mysterious fevers off and on for about three weeks after each operation on his hand. Fevers sometimes did that to him: excited his imagination.

He lived four blocks from the school. The school bus dropped him off at his corner. In his schoolbag he carried his books and the notebook with the drawing.

His mother offered him a snack, but he said he wasn't hungry. Up in his room, he looked again at the drawing and was astonished to discover that the zebra had reached the edge of his name and appeared poised to leap off.

It *had* to be a fever that was causing him to see the zebra that way. And sure enough, when his mother took his temperature, the thermometer registered 102.6 degrees.

She gave him his medicine, but it didn't seem to have much effect, because when he woke at night and switched on his desk light and peered at the drawing, he saw the little zebra galloping across the page, along the contours of his face, over the hills and valleys of his eyes and nose and mouth, and he heard the tiny clickings of its hooves as cloudlets of dust rose in its wake.

He knew he was asleep. He knew it was the fever working upon his imagination.

But it was so real.

The little zebra running…

When he woke in the morning the fever was gone, and the zebra was quietly in its place over ADAM.

Later, as he entered the school, he noticed a large sign on the bulletin board in the hallway:

SUMMER ART CLASS

The well-known American artist Mr. John Wilson will

conduct an art class during the summer for students in 7th and 8th grades. For details, speak to Mrs. English. There will be no tuition fee for this class.

During the morning, between classes, Zebra ran into Mrs. English in the second-floor hallway.

"Mrs. English, about the summer art class...is it okay to ask where—um—where Mr. Wilson is from?"

"He is from a small town in Virginia. Are you thinking of signing up for his class?"

"I can't draw," Zebra said.

"Drawing is something you can learn."

"Mrs. English, is it okay to ask how did Mr. Wilson—um—get hurt?"

The school corridors were always crowded between classes. Zebra and Mrs. English formed a little island in the bustling, student-jammed hallway.

"Mr. Wilson was wounded in the war in Vietnam," Mrs. English said. "I would urge you to join his class. You will get to use your imagination."

For the next hour, Zebra sat impatiently through Mr. Morgan's geography class, and afterward he went up to the teacher.

"Mr. Morgan, could I—um—ask where is Vietnam?"

Mr. Morgan smoothed down the jacket of his beige summer suit, touched his bow tie, rolled down a wall map, picked up his pointer, and cleared his throat.

"Vietnam is this long, narrow country in southeast Asia, bordered by China, Laos, and Cambodia. It is a land of valleys in the north, coastal plains in the center, and marshes in the south. There are barren mountains and tropical rain forests. Its chief crops are rice, rubber, fruits, and vegetables. The population numbers close to seventy million people. Between 1962 and 1973, America fought a terrible war there to prevent the south from falling into the hands of the communist north. We lost the war."

"Thank you."

"I am impressed by your suddenly awakened interest in geography, young man, though I must remind you that your class is studying the Mediterranean," said Mr. Morgan.

During the afternoon recess, Zebra was watching a heated basketball game, when he looked across the yard and saw John Wilson walk by, carrying a laden plastic bag. Some while later, he came back along the street, empty-handed.

Over supper that evening, Zebra told his parents he was thinking of taking a summer art class offered by the school.

His father said, "Well, I think that's a fine idea."

"Wait a minute. I'm not so sure," his mother said.

"It'll get him off the streets," his father said. "He'll become a Matisse instead of a lawyer like his dad. Right, Adam?"

"Just you be very careful," his mother said to Adam. "Don't do anything that might injure your hand."

"How can drawing hurt his left hand, for heaven's sake?" said his father.

That night, Zebra lay in bed looking at his hand. It was a dread and a mystery to him, his own hand. The fingers were all there, but like dead leaves that never fell, the ring and little fingers were rigid and curled, the others barely moved. The doctors said it would take time to bring them back to life. So many broken bones. So many torn muscles and tendons. So many injured nerves. The dark shadow had sprung upon him so suddenly. How stupid, stupid, *stupid* he had been!

He couldn't sleep. He went over to his desk and looked at John Wilson's drawing. The galloping little zebra stood very still over ADAM.

Early the following afternoon, on the last day of school, Zebra went to Mrs. English's office and signed up for John Wilson's summer art class.

"The class will meet every weekday from ten in the morning until one," said Mrs. English. "Starting Monday."

Zebra noticed the three plastic bags in a corner of the office.

"Mrs. English, is it okay to ask what Mr. Wilson—um—did in Vietnam?"

"He told me he was a helicopter pilot," Mrs. English said. "Oh, I neglected to mention that you are to bring an unlined notebook and a pencil to the class."

"That's all? A notebook and a pencil?"

Mrs. English smiled. "And your imagination."

When Zebra entered the art class the next Monday morning, he found about fifteen students there—including Andrea from his class with Mrs. English.

The walls of the room were bare. Everything had been removed for the summer. Zebra noticed two plastic bags on the floor beneath the blackboard.

He sat down at the desk next to Andrea's.

She wore blue jeans and a yellow summer blouse with blue stripes. Her long red hair was tied behind her head with a dark-blue ribbon. She gazed at Zebra through her thick glasses, leaned over, and said, "Are you going to make gloomy drawings, too?"

Just then John Wilson walked in, carrying a plastic bag, which he put down on the floor next to the two others.

He stood alongside the front desk, wearing a light-blue long-sleeved shirt and jeans. The left shirtsleeve had been folded back and pinned to the shirt. The dark-blue cap with the words LAND ROVER sat jauntily on his head.

"Good morning to you-all," he said, with a shy smile. "Mighty glad you're here. We're going to do two things this summer. We're going to make paper into faces and garbage into people. I can see by your expressions that you don't know what I'm talking about, right? Well, I'm about to show you."

He asked everyone to draw the face of someone sitting nearby.

Zebra hesitated, looked around, then made a drawing of Andrea. Andrea carefully drew Zebra.

He showed Andrea his drawing.

"It's awful." She grimaced. "I look like a mouse."

Her drawing of him was good. But was his face really so sad?

John Wilson went from desk to desk, peering intently at the drawings. He paused a long moment over Zebra's drawing. Then he spent more than an hour demonstrating with chalk on the blackboard how they should not be thinking *eyes* or *lips* or *hands* while drawing, but should think only *lines* and *curves* and *shapes*; how they should be looking at where everything was situated in relation to the edge of the paper; and how they should not be looking *directly* at the edges of what they were drawing but at the space *outside* the edges.

Zebra stared in wonder at how fast John Wilson's hand

raced across the blackboard, and at the empty sleeve rising and falling lightly against the shirt.

"You-all are going to learn how to *see* in a new way," John Wilson said.

They made another drawing of the same face.

"Now I look like a horse," Andrea said. "Are you going to add stripes?"

"You are one big pain, Andrea," Zebra said.

Shortly before noon, John Wilson laid out on his desk the contents of the plastic bags: a clutter of junked broken objects, including the doll and the umbrella.

Using strips of cloth, some lengths of string, crumpled newspaper, his pen, and his one hand, he swiftly transformed the battered doll into a red-nosed, umbrella-carrying clown, with baggy pants, a tattered coat, a derby hat, and a somber smile. Turning over the battered frying pan, he made it into a pedestal, on which he placed the clown.

"That's a sculpture," John Wilson said, with his shy smile. "Garbage into people."

The class burst into applause. The clown on the frying pan looked as if it might take a bow.

"You-all will be doing that, too, before we're done," John Wilson said. "Now I would like you to sign and date your drawings and give them to me."

When they returned the next morning the drawings were on a wall.

Gradually, in the days that followed, the walls began to fill with drawings. Sculptures made by the students were looked at with care, discussed by John Wilson and the class, and then placed on shelves along the walls: a miniature bicycle made of wire; a parrot made of an old sofa cushion; a cowboy made of rope and string; a fat lady made of a dented metal pitcher; a zebra made of glued-together scraps of cardboard.

"I like your zebra," Andrea said.

"Thanks," Zebra said. "I like your parrot."

One morning John Wilson asked the class members to make a contour drawing of their right or left hand. Zebra felt himself sweating and trembling as he worked.

"That's real nice," John Wilson said, when he saw Andrea's drawing.

He gazed at the drawing made by Zebra.

"You-all were looking at your hand," he said. "You ought to have been looking at the edge of your hand and at the space outside."

Zebra drew his hand again. Strange and ugly, the two fingers lay rigid and curled. But astonishingly, it looked like a hand this time.

One day, a few minutes before the end of class, John Wilson gave everyone an assignment: draw or make something at home, something very special that each person *felt deeply* about. And bring it to class.

Zebra remembered seeing a book titled *Incredible Cross-Sections* on a shelf in the family room at home. He found the book and took it into his room.

There was a color drawing of a rescue helicopter on one of the Contents pages. On pages 30 and 31, the helicopter was shown in pieces, its complicated insides displayed in detailed drawings. Rotor blades, control rods, electronics equipment, radar scanner, tail rotor, engine, lifeline, winch—all its many parts.

Zebra sat at his desk, gazing intently at the space outside the edges of the helicopter on the Contents page.

He made an outline drawing and brought it to class the next morning.

John Wilson looked at it. Was there a stiffening of his muscular neck, a sudden tensing of the hand that held the drawing?

He took the drawing and tacked it to the wall.

The next day he gave them all the same home assignment: draw or make something they *felt very deeply* about.

That afternoon, Zebra went rummaging through the trash bin in his kitchen and the garbage cans that stood near the back door of his home. He found some sardine cans, a broken egg-beater, pieces of cardboard, chipped buttons, bent bobby pins, and other odds and ends.

With the help of epoxy glue, he began to make of those bits of garbage a kind of helicopter. For support, he used his desk-top, the floor, his knees, the elbow of his left arm, at one point even his chin. Struggling with the last piece—a button he wanted to position as a wheel—he realized that without thinking he had been using his left hand, and the two curled fingers had straightened slightly to his needs.

His heart beat thunderously. There had been so many hope-filled moments before, all of them ending in bitter disappointment. He would say nothing. Let the therapist or the doctors tell him....

The following morning, he brought the helicopter to the class.

"Eeewwww, what is *that*?" Andrea grimaced.

"Something to eat you with," Zebra said.

"Get human, Zebra. Mr. Wilson will have a laughing fit over that."

But John Wilson didn't laugh. He held the helicopter in his hand a long moment, turning it this way and that, nodded at Zebra, and placed it on a windowsill, where it shimmered in the summer sunlight.

The next day, John Wilson informed everyone that three students would be leaving the class at the end of July. He asked each of those students to make a drawing for him that he would get to keep. Something to remember them by. All their other drawings and sculptures they could take home.

Zebra lay awake a long time that night, staring into the darkness of his room. He could think of nothing to draw for John Wilson.

In the morning, he sat gazing out the classroom window at the sky and at the helicopter on the sill.

"What are you going to draw for him?" Andrea asked.

Zebra shrugged and said he didn't know.

"Use your imagination," she said. Then she said, "Wait, what am I seeing here? Are you able to move those fingers?"

"I think so."

"You *think* so?"

"The doctors said there was some improvement."

Her eyes glistened behind the thick lenses. She seemed genuinely happy.

He sat looking out the window. Dark birds wheeled and soared. There was the sound of traffic. The helicopter sat on the windowsill, its eggbeater rotor blades ready to move to full throttle.

Later that day, Zebra sat at his desk at home, working on a

drawing. He held the large sheet of paper in place by pressing down on it with the palm and fingers of his left hand. He drew a landscape: hills and valleys, forests and flatlands, rivers and plateaus. Oddly, it all seemed to resemble a face.

Racing together over that landscape were a helicopter and a zebra.

It was all he could think to draw. It was not a very good drawing. He signed it: "To JOHN WILSON, with thanks. Zebra."

The next morning, John Wilson looked at the drawing and asked Zebra to write on top of the name "John Wilson" the name "Leon."

"He was an old buddy of mine, an artist. We were in Vietnam together. Would've been a much better artist than I'll ever be."

Zebra wrote in the new name.

"Thank you kindly," John Wilson said, taking the drawing. "Zebra, you have yourself a good time in camp and a good life. It was real nice knowing you."

He shook Zebra's hand. How strong his fingers felt!

"I think I'm going to miss you a little," Andrea said to Zebra after the class.

"I'll only be away a month."

"Can I help you carry some of those drawings?"

"Sure. I'll carry the helicopter."

Zebra went off to a camp in the Adirondack Mountains. He hiked and read and watched others playing ball. In the arts and crafts program he made some good drawings and even got to learn a little bit about watercolors. He put together clowns and airplanes and helicopters out of discarded cardboard and wood and clothing. From time to time his hand hurt, but the fingers seemed slowly to be coming back to life.

"Patience, young man," the doctors told him when he returned to the city. "You're getting there."

One or two additional operations were still necessary. But there was no urgency. And he no longer needed the leg brace.

On the first day of school, one of the secretaries found him in the hallway and told him to report to Mrs. English.

"Did you have a good summer?" Mrs. English asked.

"It was okay," Zebra said.

"This came for you in the mail."

She handed him a large brown envelope. It was addressed to Adam Zebrin, Eighth Grade, at the school. The sender was John Wilson, with a return address in Virginia.

"Adam, I admit I'm very curious to see what's inside," Mrs. English said.

She helped Zebra open the envelope.

Between two pieces of cardboard were a letter and a large color photograph.

The photograph showed John Wilson down on his right knee before a glistening dark wall. He wore his army jacket and blue jeans and boots, and the cap with the words LAND ROVER. Leaning against the wall to his right was Zebra's drawing of the helicopter and the zebra racing together across a facelike landscape. The drawing was enclosed in a narrow frame.

The wall behind John Wilson seemed to glitter with a strange black light.

Zebra read the letter and showed it to Mrs. English.

Dear Zebra,

One of the people whose names are on this wall was among my very closest friends. He was an artist named

Leon Kellner. Each year I visit him and leave a gift—something very special that someone creates and gives me. I leave it near his name for a few hours, and then I take it to my studio in Virginia, where I keep a collection of those gifts. All year long I work in my studio, but come summer I go looking for another gift to give him.

Thank you for your gift.

Your friend,
John Wilson

P.S. I hope your hand is healing.

Mrs. English stood staring awhile at the letter. She turned away and touched her eyes. Then she went to a shelf on the wall behind her, took down a large book, leafed through it quickly, found what she was searching for, and held it out for Zebra to see.

Zebra found himself looking at the glistening black wall of the Vietnam Memorial in Washington, D.C. And at the names on it, the thousands of names....

Later, in the schoolyard during recess, Zebra stood alone at the chain-link fence and gazed down the street toward Franklin Avenue. He thought how strange it was that all the houses on this street had seemed to turn toward John Wilson that day, the windows and porches and columns and doors, as if saluting him.

Had that been only his imagination?

Maybe, Zebra thought, just maybe he could go for a walk to Franklin Avenue on Saturday or Sunday. He had not walked along Franklin Avenue since the accident; had not gone down that steep hill. Yes, he would walk carefully down that hill to the corner and walk back up and past the school and then the four blocks home.

Andrea came over to him.

"We didn't get picked for the story class with Mrs. English," she said. "I won't have to listen to any more of your gloomy stories."

Zebra said nothing.

"You know, I think I'll walk home today instead of taking the school bus," Andrea said.

"Actually, I think I'll walk, too," Zebra said. "I was thinking maybe I could pick up some really neat stuff in the street."

"You are becoming a pleasant life form," Andrea said.

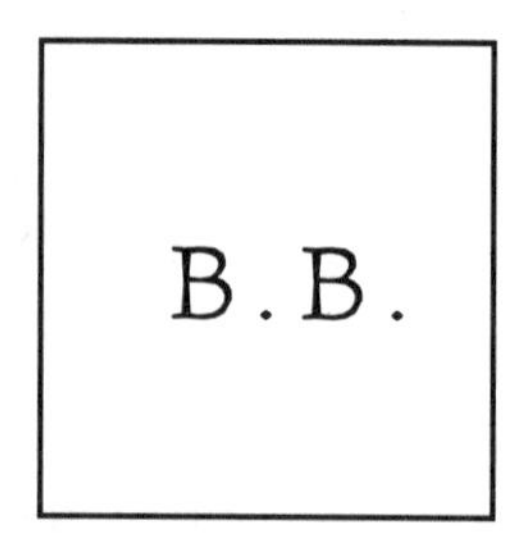

I DON'T KNOW about you, but in my family there are big secrets. Sometimes we share them; sometimes we don't. For example, Dad didn't want any more children after little Timmy died. Mom did. So she went ahead and got herself pregnant, and kept it secret until she was absolutely sure, and then told Dad one evening during supper. Dad said he didn't want to go through all that hell again with another sick child. Mom said all of life was a gamble, playing the odds. Dad said he felt deceived; he said Mom should have told him about not taking the pill. Mom said she didn't want me growing up an only child. Neither of them really paid much attention to me as they kept shouting at each other across the kitchen table.

I don't know why Mom told Dad in my presence; maybe she thought my being there might prevent a fight. I don't know why Dad got so angry; I thought having kids was what marriage was all about. I don't know what other secrets Mom has; probably plenty. Sometimes it seems to me that half of the stories in the papers and on TV are about the secrets people have, and the other half are about what they do when the secrets are uncovered.

As for Dad's big secret—I found out about it the day my new brother was born.

The night before Mom went to the hospital, the three of us were sitting in the kitchen having supper. Dad was sweating even though the house was on the cold side—Mom always kept our thermostat low to help conserve the planet's fossil fuels. I saw the sweat on his forehead and upper lip, and I thought maybe he was nervous about his business trip to New York. He finished his apple pie and sat back. Mom asked me if I was going to eat my piece of pie, and I nodded. She got up from the table and went over to the sink. She had on a below-the-knees dark-blue wool maternity dress that ballooned out over her big belly and highlighted her short, frizzy strawberry-blond hair. Her normally pale narrow face had grown round and full during her pregnancy and glowed with a ruddy color; there was a large pink island on each of her cheeks; her green eyes sparkled.

Dad looked out the window at the falling snow visible in our outdoor floodlights and covering our driveway.

"It's pretty bad out there," he said gloomily.

"If you can go to New York, I can go to the school board meeting," Mom said.

Dad's eyes darted about and fixed on a point somewhere beyond Mom's head. Mom asked us to help clean up.

Dad and I began to clear the table. He was in his late thirties, heavy-shouldered, muscular, and handsome-looking, with a smooth, pink-skinned boyish face, a straight nose, and a head of thick dark hair. He had a half-inch scar near the outside corner of his right eye: an old football injury. On a wall in their bedroom there was a picture of him in his high school football uniform; he'd been a running back, during one game rushing one hundred fifty yards in eleven carries. He told me one Sunday afternoon when we were alone—Mom was doing catch-up work in her office in town—that he'd wanted to play professional football after college. "But no team would take me," he said. "Didn't have the right stuff." He looked away from me when he said it, his eyes dark and bleak. Then he added, still not looking at me, "B.B., I've never told that to your mom. Let's keep that just between the two of us, okay?"

I was about six then. Somehow it felt good having Dad tell me that, keeping Dad's words from Mom. It felt warm and close, like we were building a tree house just for ourselves to play in. Anyway, Dad said he went on to business school and for a while worked in a bank. That was where he met Mom, who was with the firm that managed the bank's legal affairs. After they were married he went to work for a development company, where he was now project director. He didn't seem very happy with his job—he worked long hours and did lots of traveling—though he was successful at it. Most of the kids in my class at school said their fathers weren't happy with their jobs, so I didn't think there was anything unusual about Dad's feelings.

We finished cleaning up. Some minutes later, Dad stood at the front door, hatless and wearing his high-collared olive-green belted winter coat. He looked like a TV journalist going off to a war. He kissed my cheek. "Take care of yourself, B.B.," he said to me, "and don't give your mom a hard time." He leaned over Mom's belly and kissed her.

"Why're you taking your big bag?" Mom asked.

Dad said he'd packed some extra things. "A snowstorm like this, I could get stuck in New York."

He lifted the bag and went outside, pushing the door shut with a rapid sideways movement of his legs and hips.

A few minutes later, Mom came downstairs and went out the back door in her gray storm coat and long red-and-white woolen scarf and snow boots and fur cap. I saw her take the car down the driveway. Her license plate read LAW-MOM.

I should've been studying for an exam, but a kind of weird screen seemed to have risen between me and the book on my desk. I could see through the screen to the book, but the words on the pages couldn't work their way through the screen into my head.

After a while I went downstairs and took a piece of apple pie out of the fridge and made myself a cup of hot chocolate. I sat at the kitchen table, eating and drinking. The house was quiet, but I thought I could hear little Timmy crying in his bed upstairs. That made me feel cold and shivery. I finished the piece of pie and the hot chocolate. I left the lights on in the kitchen and started up the stairs.

Passing the open door to Mom and Dad's bedroom, I looked in and saw that Mom had forgotten to turn off their bathroom light. A wedge of light lay across the bedroom and angled up the wall covered with photographs of their early lives: their parents and sisters and brothers; Dad proud and grinning in his high school and college football uniforms; Mom smiling in her law school graduation cap and gown; Mom in her bridal gown and Dad in his tux at their lawn wedding, and in bathing suits on a two-masted sailboat off the coast of Maine during their honeymoon; Mom pregnant with me; me as an infant, as a five-year-old on a pony, as an angel in a school play; and little Timmy alone and with Mom and Dad and me before he became sick.

Turning to leave, I noticed the plastic case that stood open on Dad's bureau. The case had two sides. One held a color photo of me. The side that folded over the photo contained two small digital clocks for two time zones, and a recording device that could carry a message. Closed, the case was about the size of a credit card. Six months before, Dad had asked me to say something into it that he could take along with him on his business trips, and I'd said, "Daddy, I love you and miss you a lot, please come home soon." Well, he'd forgotten to take it with him this time. I felt a little hurt by that.

Back in my room, the screen that had earlier come between me and the book seemed to have vanished. I sat at my desk and looked at drawings of an amoeba ready for fission; at drawings of the fission process and the daughter cells. I looked at a picture of the twenty-three pairs of human chromosomes, and I read about the material called DNA in the chromosomes. The book said that DNA contained instructions, or genes, that produced character traits and determined how an organism developed. I'd inherited half my genes from my mother and half from my father, the book said.

I read a new section of the book, said words out loud, but kept getting them confused: diploid and haploid cells, binary fission, mitosis. I wondered whose genes, Mom's or Dad's, had caused little Timmy to die. That was another big secret in our house; no one talked about that, about genes.

Someone touched my shoulder. I sat up with a start, my heart suddenly surging. Mom. I'd left my door open. She'd removed her coat and hat and boots. Her cheeks were flushed with cold, and her hair was in disarray.

"It's very late," she said.

"I'm almost done studying."

"Don't tell your dad I got home so late. Did he call?"

I said no, Dad hadn't called.

"His train may have been delayed by the snow." She put her hands on her belly. "Your new brother is really kicking tonight. Here, feel."

I placed my hand on her enormous belly and felt him move.

"What're you studying?" she asked.

"Cells and genes and stuff."

She stood quietly a long moment, gazing at the book on my desk. Then she said, "Darling, I'm very tired and I'm going to bed. How about pancakes and hot chocolate in the morning? Does that sound okay? Good night, sweet. Don't stay up too late."

She bent to kiss my cheek. The feel of her lips sent a shiver through me. Dry. Chapped. Little Timmy's lips.

I woke to the radio. My eyes still closed, I lay very still, hoping the announcer would say school had been canceled because of the snowstorm. Instead, I heard news about the war in Bosnia and a bus bombing in Jerusalem.

It was cold in the house: Mom and her determination to save the planet. I showered and dressed and went downstairs to the warm odors in the kitchen.

Mom was wearing her fleece-lined bedroom slippers and yellow bathrobe, and she looked huge-bellied and weary. Her hair was barely combed, her eyes were red-rimmed, puffy. She stood near the stove, making pancakes, one hand over the griddle, the other resting on her hip. "Good morning," she said, with no attempt at cheer. "Please set the table and pour the orange juice. Are you sure your dad didn't call last night? Could the phone have rung while you were in the bathroom?"

"No, Mom. Besides, Dad would've left a message."

We ate breakfast and I helped her clean up. I settled the schoolbag on my shoulders.

"Come straight home after school," she said, her lips brushing my cheek.

Outside, the powdery snow squeaked under my boots. A plow had come through; hillocks of snow lay along both sides of the street. The air was cold, the sun dazzling.

Seth Walker and Phoebe Degan were waiting at the corner. "Hey," Phoebe said to me. "Are you ready for the exam?"

Seth blew bubble gum into the air, held the small pink balloon on his lips a moment, and sucked it in.

"You moron, you'll get the worst case of chapped lips," Phoebe said. Her oval face, with its high cheekbones and thick lips, wore its usual eyeliner, blusher, lipstick. She and Seth had just turned twelve and were among the cigarette smokers in the class.

"My *dad* used to keep me up nights before he split," Seth said. "Now it's Mr. Geissen. Hey, Phoebe, you got a smoke?"

"The bus'll be here in a minute, Seth."

He started another bubble, but it burst and splattered across his lips.

I saw our yellow-and-black school bus turn a corner two blocks away. It pulled up and we climbed aboard.

The bus was about half full. I found a window seat, and Seth sat down next to me. He was short, bony, thin-shouldered, and far beyond his years in meanness. The sunlight that shone into the bus fell on his silver earring.

"You study?" he asked.

"I tried."

"You understand this stuff?"

I shook my head.

He stared out the window. "Man, I wish I had a smoke," he said.

The bus arrived at the school. We were walking to the building, when I saw Beth Silverstone heading toward us, her blond ponytail bobbing up and down.

"Hey, Mr. Geissen won't be in school today," she said. "The exam's been postponed."

"What happened?" Phoebe asked.

"Someone in his family got sick," said Beth.

"I'll bet it's his son's boyfriend," Seth said, suddenly grinning.

"Seth, you are very definitely genetically handicapped," Phoebe said.

The teacher who substituted for Mr. Geissen was a balding man with small eyes and a high voice. He wore a plaid jacket with elbow patches, baggy trousers, and a button-down shirt without a tie. I sat in the classroom paying no attention to what he was saying and thinking instead of my mom and her big belly and of my dad in New York and of Mr. Geissen, a trim man in his forties, standing at the blackboard and explaining the DNA ladder to us—when the voice of Mrs. Maklin, the school secretary, came through the intercom, summoning me to the office. I got shakily to my feet. Every eye in the class turned to look at me.

I hurried through the hallway and down the stairs and along the first-floor corridor. In the office, Mrs. Maklin told me that my mom had gone to University Hospital to have her baby. I was to spend the night with Mrs. Watson, our neighbor across the street. Mrs. Watson was a spry lady in her late sixties. Her children were married and lived out of the city. Her husband had died about two weeks after little Timmy.

In the hallway after class, I told Phoebe and Seth about my mom. Phoebe said, "Hey, not to worry." Seth said, grinning, "Now you get to not sleep nights for at least a whole year." To which Phoebe said, "Whose mean gene did you inherit, Seth?"

The rest of the school day I could think only of Mom in the hospital alone. She'd probably called Dad, and he'd be on his way home. On the school bus, it occurred to me that if Dad was returning, why did I have to spend the night in Mrs. Watson's house?

I walked quickly from the corner bus stop. The air was so cold it hurt to breathe. Inside the house, I turned up the thermostat and checked the answering machine. There was a call from Grandma, Mom's mom, asking how Mom was, made before she'd gone to the hospital. Nothing from Dad.

I called Grandma and left a message on her answering machine. Then I phoned Mrs. Watson and said I wanted to stay in my own house overnight. "No, dear," she said. "Pack some things and come here. You'll stay with me."

"But isn't my dad coming home today?"

"I have no idea. But you should do as your mother says. This isn't a time to worry her."

"I'll finish my homework and then I'll come over."

"That's fine, dear. There'll be a nice supper waiting for you."

I spent about an hour on my homework and nearly another hour going over the book for Mr. Geissen's exam.

All that time, the phone didn't ring. Finally, I couldn't stand the silence, and I got up and wandered around the house and went into my parents' bedroom. I had to admit to myself that they really fought in there, really yelled at each other a lot. Once, I'd heard something crash and Mom shouting, "Go ahead, go ahead, I dare you!" It always scared me to hear them yelling like that, but I never said anything about it. A lot of kids in my class said their parents shouted at each other, so I thought it was pretty normal. But it being normal didn't make it any less scary for me. Anyway, now the room was quiet. The whole house was quiet, eerily quiet; I kept thinking that something would jump out at me from the shadows like in one of those horror movies. I looked at the pictures on the wall and noticed the plastic case on the dresser, the one with the photo of me and the recording device and the two clocks, the one Dad usually took along with him on his trips but had left behind this time. I picked it up and touched the Play button, thinking I'd like hearing my voice break the heavy silence in the house, and instead I suddenly heard Dad's voice saying, "B.B., I'm going to ask your mom to point you to this message. By the time you get to it, you'll already have heard from your mom that I've left her. Yes, I'm leaving. I've thought about this for a very long time. You remember what it was like with Timmy. I know for sure I don't have the heart and the strength to go through all that again. I just can't do it. Please try to understand that this doesn't mean I don't love you. I love you with all my heart. But I'm not going to be any good for you or for your mom these next years. I'm really sorry to be telling you this through a recording, but I just can't face you or your mom right now. All I can see and hear right now is little Timmy. All my love, your dad."

His voice sounded rushed and quivery, and I was so sure he was in the room that I turned, expecting to see him. But all I saw was the large bed with its flowery spread and Mom's lawbooks on her night table and Dad's sports magazines on his. I pushed the Play button again, hoping I'd dreamed Dad's voice; it was my voice I'd hear, saying how much I loved and missed my dad and would he please come home soon. But I heard Dad's voice again. I listened to his words, and then I heard the panic in my heart and saw my hands trembling. I put the plastic case back on the dresser and went out of the room. Still trembling, I packed some things. In the bathroom, I peed and washed my hands and face and stared into the mirror and saw Dad's face looking out at me. Smooth, pink-skinned; a straight nose; a head of thick dark hair. Little Timmy's face before he became sick. I went out of the house and crossed the street to Mrs. Watson's.

She must've been watching for me from her front window, because she opened her door before I even rang the bell. "No news from your mom yet," she said.

I cried a lot that night and didn't sleep much. In school the next day, Mr. Geissen was still not back. My classmates kept asking how Mom was feeling and would she and Dad throw a party for the class. All their words sounded as if they were coming through a wall. At times I felt I was standing a long way outside myself, watching and listening without interest to what was happening to me. Once, in class, I looked down and saw my hands shaking and was very frightened. At one point during the day, I astonished myself by suddenly asking Seth why his parents had divorced. His face turned a deep red, and he said furiously, "None of your business, amoeba brain." I thought he would punch me or something, that's how angry he looked. But he took two or three deep breaths and finally said, "Because of my dad's drinking. He tried to keep it from us, but we all knew."

By the time he finished telling me that, there were tears in his eyes. He turned and walked quickly away.

After school I went to Mrs. Watson's house. As soon as she opened the door, she said, "Your mom gave birth to a boy. I'll be very happy to drive you to the hospital. Would you like some hot chocolate and apple pie before we go?"

Because of the heavy traffic on the expressway, the drive took a long time. It was some while before Mrs. Watson found a parking space in the hospital garage. She backed carefully into it and we climbed out and she locked the car.

"The elevators are over there, dear. I know my way around this hospital. I had four children here and visited my late husband every day when he was ill, Lord rest his soul."

We took the garage elevator to the main floor and got out and walked to another elevator. It was crowded with doctors and visitors.

Mrs. Watson took my hand as we arrived at our floor and led me past the nurses' station and along a quiet corridor to a closed door. There were nurses and orderlies in the corridor, metal tables and wheelchairs. Mrs. Watson asked me to wait a moment and went inside. In less than a minute she was back, telling me to go into the room.

Inside were three beds. A dark-haired woman about Mom's age lay angled upward in the far bed, looking out the window at the winter night. Her stomach was flat, and she was crying quietly. The middle bed was empty. Mom lay in the bed nearest the door. She wore a pink nightgown. Her hair was combed, her lips were chapped, and her face was pale.

In the bed with Mom was my new brother.

"Hello, darling," Mom said, in an exhausted voice. "Come here and meet your brother."

She was holding him to her breast. He lay wrapped in a blue flannel blanket and had on a white pointed woolen cap with a pom-pom. I saw his tiny fingers and small lips and the smooth pink curve of his face. His eyes were closed. He was the size of a doll.

"See, he's trying to nurse," Mom said. "But my milk won't come in for another day or two."

"Is he okay?" I asked.

"The doctor says he's fine," Mom said.

"Will he get sick like Timmy?"

"We have to wait and see," Mom said. "Come here and sit on the bed."

I sat down and kissed her cheek. Her face was dry and smooth. My new brother stirred, screwed up his face, opened his eyes. His irises were a watery blue.

"Did Dad call?" Mom asked.

I stared at her, bewildered, and said no.

Mom said, "I phoned his office and left a message that I was going to the hospital."

I felt faint with confusion and panic, and needed to take some quick deep breaths.

Mom said, "I wonder why he hasn't called."

I sat on the bed, hoping she wouldn't feel my trembling. After a while I could tell she was getting tired. Finally, she said, "It's best that you go now, darling. The nurse will be coming soon for the baby."

Mrs. Watson was waiting for me in the corridor. "Isn't he a beautiful baby?" she said.

I walked with her to the elevators. Standing there, I realized I'd forgotten to ask Mom how long she'd be in the hospital. I asked Mrs. Watson, but she didn't know. I said, "Could I ask my mom?" and Mrs. Watson said, "Why, of course, dear."

I hurried back to the room and entered without thinking to knock and saw Mom in the bed, one arm over her eyes, the other cradling my little brother, and tears were running down her cheeks. She hadn't heard me enter. I stood there for a long moment, my knees weak and my heart pounding. Then I backed out of the room and quietly closed the door.

Inside the crowded elevator, all I could see was Mom lying in the bed, holding my baby brother and crying. Maybe she was thinking of little Timmy. Maybe she was wondering about Dad, suddenly realizing that he'd left us. I should've told her about his message. I should go back up now and tell her. How could I not tell her? How could I let her spend the night here not knowing that? I turned to Mrs. Watson, wanting to say, "I need to go back up and see my mom about something important." But just then the elevator stopped and the door opened and Mrs. Watson took my hand and led me into a crowd of people—and right there stood Dad!

He was gazing over my head and didn't see me at first. I felt a strange lightness surge into my head, and it seemed for a second that all the sounds around me had suddenly vanished, like someone hitting the Low on a volume control. If Mrs. Watson hadn't been holding my hand, I would've fallen, that's how astounded I felt at the unexpected sight of my dad. Then he saw me, and his eyes lit up. He let the crowd go past him into the elevator and bent and wrapped his arms around me and lifted me off my feet. He wore his high-collared olive-green belted winter coat and smelled of cold air. The bouquet of purple and yellow flowers he was carrying brushed against my face. Planting a kiss on my cheek, he said exuberantly, "I just got back. We have a new baby! Isn't that wonderful?"

I stood there and stared at him, feeling a little dazed and listening to the rush of blood in my ears.

"Mom's very tired," I heard myself say.

"I'll bet she is! How are you, Mrs. Watson?"

"I'm just fine."

"Say, are these flowers okay, do you think?"

"They're lovely," said Mrs. Watson.

He grinned and started for one of the elevators, then stopped. It was headed down to the basement. The door to a second elevator opened, and he stepped inside. As the door slid shut, I saw him looking at me. His eyes darted away and fixed on a point behind my head.

Outside, it had begun to snow again. Mrs. Watson drove

home slowly. As we got out of her car, she said, "I think you can sleep in your own house tonight."

I went directly to my parents' bedroom. Dad's large suitcase was lying closed on the bed. I took the plastic case off the bureau and switched on the recording device, and I heard only an empty hiss. I put the case back on the bureau and went to my room.

The next day, Mr. Geissen was back in school. He sat behind his desk, wearing a white turtleneck sweater and a dark-blue blazer and gray trousers. In his soft voice, he said, "There is a man named Robert, who is quite ill, and these days I find it difficult to speak his name without feeling an enormous sadness, because I know that the person attached to the name will soon be gone."

For the next two days, Mr. Geissen was away from school. The man named Robert had died.

Mr. Geissen gave us the exam the day he returned. At one point during the exam, I looked up and saw him seated behind the desk, dabbing at his eyes with a handkerchief. I imagined him at a bedside, gazing down with hopeless desperation at a shrunken face. Later, in the bus, Seth told me that the man Mr. Geissen had talked about was his son. He stared past me out the window as he said it. His face looked shockingly pale.

Mom had come home from the hospital two days after she gave birth. Some nights later, she and Dad were in their bedroom. Mom lay on her side of the large bed and Dad sat on the edge. The house was warm. Mom was letting me hold my new brother. His crib stood near their bed, and I sat in a chair next to it. He was so small and light. His lips were moist, his face was smooth and pink. He smelled of talcum and baby lotion. They'd named him Eric, after Mom's dad. He looked like Mom. I held him and hoped he'd be okay. I hoped he wouldn't start crying one day and not stop. I hoped his face wouldn't become old-looking. I hoped he wouldn't stop eating and growing. I hoped I would never see Dad trying to hold him and calm him and then stare at him with revulsion and put him down in his bed and go off and turn his face to the wall and cry—all the while not knowing I was watching from the doorway.

Mom and Dad weren't talking. I saw Dad get to his feet and go to his bureau. He brought the plastic case over to me.

"Going off on a trip tomorrow," he said cheerfully, "and seem to have accidentally erased your message. Do a new one for me?"

He pressed the Record button and raised the plastic case to a few inches before my lips. Through the thundering noise in my head, I heard myself say, "Hello, Daddy. Mom and Eric and I love you and miss you a lot. Please, please, come home."

He touched the Stop button and looked at me for what seemed a long moment. "Let's check if we got that," he said, with that same cheerfulness, and pressed the Play button.

The bedroom filled with the shaky, urgent tone of a girl saying, "Hello, Daddy. Mom and Eric and I love you and miss you a lot. Please, please, come home."

I saw Dad looking at me as he touched the Stop button. Then his eyes moved away from my face and fixed on a point somewhere behind my head.

My recorded voice had startled little Eric. I felt him suddenly stiffen in my arms. He began to cry. He hadn't been crying much since he'd left the hospital.

Dad stood there looking at some point behind my head and listening to little Eric cry.

"Let me have him," Mom said. "He's probably hungry."

"Thanks for the new message, B.B.," said Dad.

These days, Eric is often sick, but the doctor says it's only the usual colds and coughs that babies get. Dad travels a lot. Each time he goes off on a trip, I think he won't come home. Sometimes I tell myself that his message is too much of a secret for me to be carrying alone. But I don't know anyone I can tell it to.

Moon

MOON VINTEN, RECENTLY turned thirteen, was short for his age and too bony, too thin. He had a small pale face, dark angry eyes, and straight jet-black hair. A tiny silver ring hung from the lobe of his right ear, and a ponytail sprouted below the thick band at the nape of his neck and ran between his angular shoulder blades. The ponytail, emerging like a waterfall from the flat-combed dark hair, was dyed the clear blue color of a morning sky.

Moon marched into the family den one autumn evening and announced to his parents that he wanted to build a recording studio for himself and his band.

His parents, short, slender people in their late forties, had been talking quietly on the sofa. Moon's father, annoyed by his son's brusque interruption of the conversation, thought: First, those drums; then the earring and the ponytail. And now a *recording studio*? In a restrained tone, he asked, "What, exactly, does that involve?"

"A big table, microphones, stands, extension cords, rugs or carpets for soundproofing, a mixing board," said Moon.

"And how will you pay for all that?"

"With the money I got for my birthday."

Patience is the desired mode here, Moon's father told himself. "I'll remind you again. That money has been put away for your college tuition."

"The band will make lots of money, Dad."

"Then buy the equipment with that money."

"We'll need money to buy the equipment so we can make really high-quality recordings," said Moon, trying to keep himself calm. "We'll demo the recordings and send them out, and start making money from the gigs we'll get. It takes money to make money, Dad."

Moon's father turned to Moon's mother. "Where is he learning these things, Julia?"

"He's your son, too, Kenneth," said Moon's mother. "Why don't you ask him?" Her mind at that moment was on another matter: the face of a boy in Pakistan.

"He's only thirteen years old, for God's sake," Moon's father said.

Moon hated it when they talked about him as if he weren't there. His parents, who were physicians, spoke often to each other clinically about their patients, and at times about Moon as if he were a patient. It was one more irritant in the list of things that made him angry.

"We shouldn't attach an 'only' to a thirteen-year-old," said his mother, still seeing the face of the Pakistani boy, whose photograph had come to her office in the morning mail. "A thirteen-year-old is not a child."

Moon's father, a precise man with a dry, intimidating manner, looked at Moon and asked, "Where, exactly, do you plan to put all that equipment?"

"In the garage," Moon replied.

His parents stared at him. Calm is called for, his father thought, and remained silent. Inside Moon's mother, an unassuming woman of gentle demeanor, the picture of the gaunt, brown-faced Pakistani boy—dry thin lips, small straight nose, enormous frightened eyes—abruptly winked out.

She said quietly to Moon, "Dear, we keep our cars in the garage."

Moon said, "Then I'll put it in the basement."

"We've been through all that," said Moon's father—the clamor erupting from the basement and streaming through the air ducts and filling the house with that booming drumming twanging pandemonium they called music. "Let's talk about it another time."

"When, Dad?"

"Soon."

"But when?"

His father said, "Morgan, I have very important calls to make." Morgan was Moon's given name, first on the list of things that made him angry. A jovial older cousin had called him Moon some years ago, for a reason Moon could no longer remember. His parents and his teachers still called him Morgan.

"I need the phone to call the guys in the band," said Moon.

"Whoever is on the phone, if an overseas call comes in on call waiting, please tell me immediately," said Moon's mother.

"I need the phone," said Moon again.

"Don't you have any homework?" his father asked.

"Dad, I really really really need to talk to the guys in my band," said Moon.

Moon's parents sat very quietly on the couch, looking at

their son. Even excited or angered, his face retained its pallid look. But his dark eyes glittered, and his thin lips drew back tight over his small white teeth as if keeping a seal on a poisonous boil of words.

The telephone rang.

Moon's father picked up the receiver and said crisply, "Dr. Vinten." He listened and handed the receiver to Moon's mother. "Pakistan," he said.

Moon, his hands clenched, turned and left the den.

He took the carpeted stairs two at a time to the second floor, and as he threw open the door to his room, the anger erupted. His heart raced, his hands shook. He felt the rage like a scalding second skin. He slammed the door shut. The large color photograph of the Beatles, tacked loosely to the inside of the door, fluttered briefly; the Beatles seemed to be dancing and undulating in their costumes.

He flopped down on his bed.

Always with the fury came fear. Occasional tantrums had accompanied him through childhood and in recent years had become too-frequent fits of rage that rose suddenly from deep inside him and sometimes took possession of his body. He lay on his back, tight and quivering. "When you feel it coming, stop what you're doing," Mrs. Graham, the school counselor, had advised. "Take deep breaths and count slowly." He counted: One...two...three...Mrs. Graham was a round-faced, good-hearted woman. "If you feel you're losing control, walk out of the classroom. I've told your teachers it's all right for you to do that." Four...five...six...It was after his fight with Tim Wesley two weeks before, when they pummeled each other and tumbled down the wide staircase into the school's main entrance hall. Seven...eight...nine...Later, Moon couldn't remember why the fight had begun. His parents and Mrs. Graham had discussed the possibility of Moon getting help. A therapist, a total stranger. Everything he'd say would be written down, probably recorded. Ten...eleven...twelve...Maybe go up to the third floor and play the drums awhile. But he needed the telephone.

Was that someone at the door?

He got down off the bed and pulled the door open and saw his mother standing in the hallway.

She said gently, "I keep reminding you, if you close your door, we can't communicate with you. Closed doors often turn into stone walls."

His mother's frequent moralizing was definitely on the list of things that made Moon angry. "Can I use the phone now?" he asked.

She sighed. "I came up to tell you that we'll be having a guest."

"Who?" asked Moon.

"A boy from Pakistan."

Children with rare diseases came to his parents from all over the world for diagnosis and treatment. But always to the hospital, never to the house.

He asked, "Why is he staying with us if he's sick?"

His mother said, "He's not sick, dear. An organization your father and I belong to is bringing him into the country. You'll hear about it in school."

"He's coming to my school?"

"Yes. Be nice to him, dear."

But Moon was imagining the boy wandering around the house and coming upon the small room on the third floor. He took a deep breath and said, "Can I use the phone now, Mom?"

Moon's mother remembered when her second son had gone off to college the year before. "It's difficult to let go, but it's much worse to hold on," she had said to Moon's father, and Moon, listening nearby, had suddenly and unaccountably run up to his room and slammed his door shut with such force that, to the disquiet of his father, the paint cracked near the ceiling on the hallway wall. She now gazed sadly at her youngest son, so different from the ambitious older ones: Andrew in engineering and football; Colin in pre-med and crew. And Morgan—so edgy and sullen, so fixed upon himself.

"Yes, dear, you may use the phone," she said. She was still standing in the hallway, looking at Moon, when he closed the door.

He sat at his cluttered desk and dialed the telephone. Pete's father answered. "Peter is doing his homework," he said.

"This won't take long, Mr. Weybridge. I promise," said Moon.

"You just make sure of that," said Pete's father.

While waiting for Pete to come to the phone, Moon sat looking at the large photographs on the wall across from his bed: John Bonham and Stewart Copeland, playing the drums. And at the photographs on the wall near his bed: George and Paul with their guitars; Ringo at his drums; John singing. He imagined himself sauntering over to them and taking the sticks from Ringo and starting with a light *tik tik tik tik* on the Hi-Hat, and then—

"Hey, hey," came Pete's voice over the phone. "How you doin', Moon?"

"We can jam after school tomorrow, Pete."

"That's cool."

"Hey, Pete, there's a kid from Pakistan who's going to be staying in my house."

"He's stayin' with *you*? Hey, that's real cool!"

"You know about him?"

"Everybody knows."

"How come I never heard anything about him?"

"Hey, you're asleep half the time. And the other half, you're so angry you don't know what's happenin'."

"I need to call Ronnie and John about tomorrow."

"Stay cool, Moon," said Pete.

Moon called Ronnie Klein and then John Wood. Just as he was telling John the time of their jam session, he heard the beep of the call waiting and told John to hang up. Another item on the list of things that angered him: the way call waiting broke into his conversations with his only friends, the members of his band. The low beep, once, twice; most of the calls were for his parents. They wouldn't give him his own telephone; they didn't want him talking on it hours on end; his brothers hadn't had their own telephones, and neither would he.

"This is Dr. Moraes," a voice said in a strange accent. "I am phoning from Pakistan for Dr. Julia Vinten."

"Just a minute, please," said Moon, and he opened his door and called downstairs. "Mom, it's for you."

"Thank you, dear." His mother's voice came to him from the den.

When he returned to his desk, he put the receiver to his ear and heard: "Yes, Dr. Vinten, the boy will arrive early tomorrow. He will no doubt be tired, but he is—"

Moon hung up the telephone.

He had not thought to ask his mother where the boy would sleep. In Andy's room? In Colin's room? He feared the dusky silences in the house that enlarged the absence of his brothers and magnified invisible presences like the noises the squirrels made scampering inside the walls. Moon imagined he heard his brothers' voices: they were teaching him to hold a bat, catch a hardball, throw a football, dribble a basketball; they were teasing him, calling him the skinny runt of the family; they were helping him with his homework; they were bickering with Mom and Dad over cars and girls and late nights out. The thought of the boy from Pakistan staying in the room of one of his brothers....

Feeling an outrage at his very center, Moon began counting. One...two...three...four...He inserted a Pearl Jam CD into his player—five...six...seven—and put on his earphones, then opened one of the textbooks on the desk. He tapped his index and middle fingers on the desk, *doom-d-d-ka-doom-doom-d-ka-doom-d-d-ka-doom-doom-d-ka*, playing as if he were at a drum and snare. The words in the book flickered and pulsated in the torrent of drums and music.

Moon sat slumped in the seat, dimly aware of the TV cameras and crews in the back of the crowded auditorium, the empty chairs on the stage, and the whispering among the students and teachers. School assemblies—almost always full of monotonous, preachy fake talk—were high on the list of things that annoyed Moon and made him angry.

He was especially angry that morning. Mrs. Woolsten had

raked him for not handing in the weekly English essay. She was a fat, ugly woman, with thick glasses and a voice like ice water. She wanted the essay tomorrow, and absolutely no excuses. He'd sensed the smirks of his classmates and saw out of the corner of his eye Pete's sympathetic look. He hadn't been able to think of anything to write about and, listening to Mrs. Woolsten's public scolding, had felt heat rise to his face. He'd considered walking out of the room, but instead he'd remained at his desk, counting to himself, fingers tapping silently on his knees...until the assistant principal's reedy voice came over the public address system, announcing the special assembly.

The crowd in the auditorium had fallen silent. Moon, still slumped in his seat, watched as some people emerged from the dark right wing of the stage and walked toward the chairs. The first was Dr. Whatley, the school principal; then came two men Moon didn't know, both dressed in dark suits; then a tall, brown-skinned man with glasses and wearing a baggy light-brown suit, followed by a brown-skinned boy about Moon's age but an inch or two shorter than Moon. He looked gaunt. His eyes were dark and enormous. He wore dark trousers and a sky-blue woolen sweater, a white shirt and a tie. His neck stuck out from the collar of the shirt like the neck of a plucked bird.

Behind the boy walked Moon's mother and father.

Moon watched as they all sat down in the chairs on the stage. The boy, looking tense and fearful, seemed not to know what to do with his hands. He sat on the edge of his chair, leaning forward and staring apprehensively at the crowded auditorium.

Dr. Whatley approached the podium and began to speak. Moon closed his eyes and wondered how he could convince his parents to let him build a recording studio. Maybe ask them for an addition to the garage. How much would that cost? Dr. Whatley droned on, his words amplified.

Moon felt itchy, impatient. There was a scattering of applause and some more talk.

A moment later, an odd-sounding voice filled the air, small and breathless and high, and Moon opened his eyes and saw the boy standing behind the podium, only his face and neck visible. Alongside the boy stood the brown-skinned man.

Moon vaguely recalled having heard that the boy's name was Ashraf.

The boy said something in a foreign language, and the man, who had been introduced as Mr. Khan, translated.

The boy spoke again. He was talking about someone named Mr. Malik and the dozen boys who worked in his carpet factory. He said the boys had been bought by Mr. Malik from their parents.

Bought? thought Moon. *Bought?*

The boy said that he himself had been bought at the age of five, for twelve dollars. He told of sitting on a bench fifteen hours a day as a carpet weaver with the others in a long, airless room, two weak lightbulbs burning from a ceiling fixture and the temperature often over one hundred degrees and the mud walls hot when he put his hands to them and the single window closed against carpet-eating insects. But that was better than working in a quarry, hauling and loading stones onto carts for the building of roads, or in the sporting goods factory owned by one of the many nephews of Mr. Malik, making soccer balls by hand eighty hours a week in silence and near darkness. At the carpet looms, he'd worked from six in the morning to eight at night, and sometimes around the clock, tying short lengths of thin thread to a lattice of heavy white threads. His fingers often bled, and the blood mixed with the colors of the threads.

"Look," he said, thrusting his hands palms upward across the podium, his thin wrists jutting like chicken bones from the sleeves of his sweater, and Moon—listening to the quavery words of the boy and the deep voice of Mr. Khan—tried to make out the fingers from across the length of the auditorium and could not, and he gazed at his own long, bony fingers and tapped them restlessly on his knees.

The audience was silent.

The boy went on talking in his high, breathless voice. Three weeks ago, in the village where he worked, two men in suits accompanied by two uniformed policemen had entered Mr. Malik's carpet factory and taken him away, along with four younger boys and three older ones. What a shouting Mr. Malik had raised! How dare they take away his workers, his boys? All legally acquired from their parents—he had the papers to prove it, documents signed and recorded with the proper authorities! The boy paused and then said, Was it right that children were made to labor at carpet factories, at brick and textile factories, at tanneries and steelworks? He said, People in America shouldn't buy the carpets made in his country. If the carpet makers couldn't sell their carpets, they wouldn't have any reason to use children as cheap labor.

He stopped, peering uncertainly at Mr. Khan, who nodded and smiled. The boy thanked the audience for listening to him and walked back to his chair and sat down. He put his hands on his knees and gazed at the floor. All the adults on the stage were looking at him.

There was an uneasy stirring in the audience and nervous, scattered applause.

Moon sat very still looking at the boy.

Dr. Whatley stepped to the podium and introduced one of the two strangers, who turned out to be the governor of the state. The second stranger was the head of the organization that had brought the boy to the United States. Moon didn't listen to them. Nor did he pay much attention to the brief talks given by his parents; each said something about the need to raise the consciousness of Americans. He was watching the boy, who sat on the edge of his chair, leaning forward and appearing a little lost—and wasn't it strange how right there on the stage, in front of everyone, as first the governor and then the head of the organization and then Moon's parents spoke, wasn't it strange how Ashraf had begun to tap with his fingers on his knees, lightly and silently tapping in small movements to some inner music he seemed to be hearing? Moon watched the rhythm and pattern of Ashraf's tapping, an odd sort of tempo, unlike anything Moon had ever seen before, and found himself tapping along with him. A one one one and a two and a one and a two and...

In the school lunchroom later that day, Moon was at a table with Pete and the two other members of his band when Ashraf entered with Mr. Khan. He saw them go along the food line and then carry their trays to a table and sit with some other students. Moon watched Ashraf eating and heard him respond to questions put to him by the students and translated by Mr. Khan. Where had he been born? What sort of food did he like? Had he ever heard of McDonald's or Walt Disney or Tom Hanks? Did he like rock and roll?

As the last question was translated, Ashraf's eyes grew

wide and bright, and he nodded. What was his favorite band? He said radiantly, smiling for the first time, "The Beatles," pronouncing it "Bee-ah-tles."

"He says," Mr. Khan translated, "that someone near the carpet factory played recordings of the Beatles very often and very loud." Students crowded around the table, blocking Moon's view. Someone asked who was Ashraf's favorite Beatle, and Moon heard the eager, high-voiced answer: "Ringo."

Minutes later, the crowd around Ashraf thinned, and Moon saw him drumming lightly on the table surface with a knife and fork. Next to him sat Mr. Khan, finishing his meal. About a half-dozen students stood near the table, watching Ashraf's drumming.

"Hey, man," Moon heard Pete say. "You talk to your mom and dad about the recording studio?"

"Yeah," said Moon, looking at Ashraf.

"What'd they say?"

"They're thinking about it."

"Man, that'd be so cool," said Pete. "Our own studio and everything."

Moon wished Pete would be quiet so he could see and hear more clearly Ashraf's oddly rhythmed drumming.

"What's up, man?" said Pete into the telephone later that afternoon. "I got one foot out the door."

"We can't jam today, Pete," said Moon.

"What's happenin'?"

"The kid from Pakistan and his interpreter, they're in my house, sleeping. We can't make any noise."

"He must be tired, man."

"I don't like him sleeping in Andy's bed. And the man, he's in Colin's bed."

"Hey, you know what my dad once said to me? He said, 'You have your own house, you can decide who sleeps there.'"

"We'll jam tomorrow."

"Tomorrow I got my guitar lesson. The day after."

"Okay, Pete."

"Stay cool, man."

Moon called the other two members of the band. Then he sat at the desk in his room, listening to the silence in the house. Two hours at the drums—gone. He thought of Ashraf's head on Andy's pillow. Did they carry diseases? Mom would know about that. His parents were at the hospital; and that evening they were to have dinner with Ashraf and Mr. Khan, along with the governor and the mayor. Moon would eat alone at home, as he did on occasion. He would put a CD into the stereo player in the den, fill the air with swelling, pounding music that drove away the ominous silences and muffled the occasional chittering and scurrying of the squirrels inside the walls of the house.

A noise took him from his thoughts: barely audible voices in the next room. Ashraf and Mr. Khan. Moon rose and left his room. He walked past his parents' bedroom to the door at the end of the hallway and climbed the wooden staircase to the third floor.

The sloping roof of the large stone-and-brick house left space for three small rooms beneath the angled beams: a cedar closet; a storage area for his parents' files; and, the third, the room where Moon played his drums and jammed with his band. There was barely enough space for the chairs and the music stands and the table with the CD player and the small cassette recorder they used to tape some of their sessions. The crowded room was the only place in the house where his parents would permit Moon and his band to play.

He removed the covers from his drums, sat down, popped The Police into the CD player, put on the earphones, and took up his sticks. He knew by heart Stewart Copeland's stroke and beat, and he played with deft precision. The blue-dyed ponytail moved from side to side and bobbed on his shoulders and back.

He played for some time, felt himself gliding off into the surge and crash of the drums and lifted into the cascades of thumping rhythms—and then he sensed an alien presence behind him, and he stopped and turned.

Ashraf and Mr. Khan were in the room.

Moon stared at them. He turned off the CD player and removed his earphones.

"We apologize if we are disturbing you," said Mr. Khan very politely.

"It's okay," said Moon, trying to keep the anger out of his voice. This was what he had feared most: an invasion of his most secret place! Slow, deep breaths...One...two...

Mr. Khan said, "Ashraf has asked me to tell you that your walls make sounds. He heard noises that woke him."

"Those are squirrels," said Moon. "Sometimes they get inside our walls. Usually we only hear them at night." Three... four...five...

Mr. Khan spoke to Ashraf, who nodded and responded.

"He says to tell you the walls of the factory where he worked were filled with insects and sometimes he would hear them at night."

Moon said, "We once had a nest of honeybees in one of our walls. My parents had to bring in a man who raised bees to take away the nest with the bees still in it." Why am I telling him this? Six...seven...

Ashraf listened attentively to the translation, nodding, then spoke softly.

"He says he does not know your name," said Mr. Khan.

"My name is Moon."

Mr. Khan looked puzzled.

"M-o-o-n," said Moon, spelling his name.

"Ah, yes?" said Mr. Khan. "Moon." He spoke to Ashraf, who responded.

"He asks why are you named Moon."

"It's my name, that's all," said Moon.

Mr. Khan spoke to Ashraf, who gazed intently at Moon. Dark, glittering pupils inside enormous, curious, eager eyes.

"Ashraf says he was drawn here by the sound of your drums and asks if he may speak frankly and put certain—um, how to say it?—personal questions to you."

"Personal? What do you mean, personal?"

"He says he will not be hurt if you do not answer."

"What questions?"

"First, he wishes to ask why you wear a ring in your ear."

"Why I wear the earring? I just do, that's all."

"Ashraf says he does not understand your answer."

"It makes me feel different. You know, not like everyone else."

"He asks why you dye your long hair blue."

"I saw it in a magazine."

"He says if you saw it in a magazine and are doing what others do, how does it make you different?"

Moon felt heat rising to his face. "No one else in my school does it."

"He asks if he may touch your hair."

"What?"

"May he touch your hair?"

Moon took a deep breath. All those questions, and now this. Touch my hair. Well, why not? He turned his head to the side. The ponytail swayed back and forth, dangling blue and loose from its roots of raven hair. Ashraf leaned forward, ran his fingers gently through the ponytail, touching and caressing the sky-blue strands, a look of wonder on his thin face. Then he withdrew his hand. Moon saw him examining his fingers and heard him speak softly to Mr. Khan.

"He says he likes the way your hair looks and feels," Mr. Khan said to Moon.

Moon looked at Ashraf, who smiled back at him shyly and spoke again to Mr. Khan.

"Now he asks why you play the drums."

Moon said, after a brief hesitation, "I just like to."

"He says to tell you that he plays drums because it is sometimes a good feeling to hit something."

"Yeah, I feel that way, too... sometimes."

Moon had never before talked about these matters with anyone.

"He says to thank you for your answers."

"Can I ask a question?"

"Of course."

"Why did he work in that factory? Why didn't he just run away?"

Mr. Khan translated, and Ashraf lowered his eyes as he responded.

"He says there was nowhere to run. He was hundreds of miles from his home and would have starved to death or been caught and brought back to his master and very severely beaten and perhaps chained to his workbench or sold off to work in the quarries."

"Why did his parents sell him?"

Ashraf listened to the translation and seemed to fill with shame.

"They needed the money to feed themselves and their other children."

"Does he have to go back?"

"Oh, yes. He feels obligated to return. Our organization will send him to school, and he will continue in the struggle to help other boys like him."

"Please say that I wish him good luck."

Mr. Khan translated, and Ashraf replied.

"He thanks you and asks if he may request of you a small favor."

"Sure."

"He asks if he may play your drums."

Moon, surprised, was silent. His drums! No one touched his drums, ever. He looked at Ashraf, who, after a moment, spoke again.

"He says he will not damage them," said Mr. Khan.

"Well, okay," Moon said.

Ashraf's eyes lit up as he extended his fingers toward Moon. Moon handed him his sticks and slid off the chair. Ashraf took the sticks, sat in Moon's chair, and tapped on Moon's drums. He tapped on the drums and the Hi-Hat, a bit awkwardly and with no apparent rhythm, and after a while he put down the sticks and picked up the bongos from the floor near the Hi-Hat. Holding the bongos between his knees, he began to tap out with his callused fingers and palms the odd rhythm he had played in the auditorium and lunchroom, a one one one and a two and a one and a two and...

Moon reached over and switched on the tape recorder.

Ashraf drummed on. Moon, standing next to him, felt the power and pull of the strange rhythm. Ashhraf played for some while, *dum dat, dum dat, dum dat,* and sweat formed on his brow and beads of sweat flecked off his face as he played and his fingers became a blur, *dum dat, dum dat, dum dat*— and abruptly he stopped. His eyes were like glowing coals. Sweat streamed down his brown face. He placed the bongos on the floor.

Moon switched off the recorder.

There was a silence before Ashraf spoke.

"He thanks you for the opportunity to play your drums," said Mr. Khan.

"Well, sure, it's okay, you're welcome," said Moon.

"He says you and he will probably never see each other again, but he will remember you."

Moon looked at Ashraf, who briefly spoke again.

"He says we must now leave and prepare for this evening's dinner," said Mr. Khan.

Ashraf extended his hand. Moon took it and was startled

by its boniness, its coarse, woodlike callus covering. Smiling shyly, Ashraf shook Moon's hand and then turned and left the small room, followed by Mr. Khan.

Moon rewound a portion of the tape, checked to see that it had recorded properly, and took it down to his room.

Pete asked, "Hey, you see him on TV?"

"See who?" replied Moon. They were walking up the crowded stairs to their English class.

"That kid, what's his name, Ashraf."

"Was he on TV?"

"Man, what planet you livin' on? He was on the news last night and on the *Today* show this mornin'."

"I was writing that essay for Mrs. Woolsten."

"Is he still at your house?"

"He left before I woke up," said Moon.

That evening, he sat with his parents in the den, watching a national news report that showed Ashraf speaking at a high school in Baltimore. He looked small and frightened behind the podium, but he thrust out his hands defiantly to show his fingers. Mr. Khan stood beside him, translating.

The next evening, Ashraf was seen on television appearing before a committee of Congress. He wore a dark suit and a tie, and his neck protruded from the shirt collar. He sat at a long table with Mr. Khan. Moon saw Ashraf's fingers tapping silently from time to time on the edge of the table.

One of the congressmen asked a question. Moon saw Ashraf thrust his hands toward the members of the committee, showing his fingers.

"Spunky kid," said Moon's father. "He's going back to a bad situation."

"Nothing will happen to him, Kenneth. Too many eyes are watching," said Moon's mother.

When Moon came down to breakfast the following morning, he found his father at the kitchen table, tense and upset. His mother, almost always too cheerful for Moon in the early hours of the day, looked troubled.

"What's happening?" Moon asked.

"See for yourself," said his father, and, handing Moon the morning newspaper, pointed to the final paragraph of an essay titled "Blunt Reply to Crusading Boy," on the op-ed page.

Moon read the paragraph:

> In conclusion, we hold that there is room for improvement in any society. But we feel that the present situation is acceptable the way it is. The National Assembly must not rush through reforms without first evaluating their impact on productivity and sales. Our position is that the government must avoid so-called humanitarian measures that harm our competitive advantages.

The essay was signed by someone named Imram Malik.

Moon asked, "What does it mean, Dad?"

"You're thirteen years old—what do you think it means?"

"I don't know," said Moon, afraid he understood it too well.

"They would not dare harm him," said his mother.

Moon felt a coldness in his heart, and the impotence that was the prologue to rage.

In the weeks that followed he played the recording often, at times taking it upstairs to the third floor and listening to it and remembering the darkly glittering blaze in Ashraf's eyes when he'd played the bongos. And that's where Moon was the winter night the portable telephone rang on the table where he'd set it, near the tape recorder. It was someone from Washington, D.C., calling his mother. His parents weren't home, he said, and wrote down an unfamiliar name and number. He turned off the telephone, and immediately it rang again, and a man's voice asked for his father. Moon was writing down the man's name and number when he heard the beep of the call waiting and felt himself growing angry. What was he, his parents' secretary or something? He'd come upstairs to play the drums, not to take their phone calls one after the other like that.

"Hey, Moon." It was Pete.

"Hey, Pete. What's up?"

"You heard the news, man?"

"What news?"

"It was just on TV. That Ashraf kid. He's dead."

"What?"

"He's dead, man. Run down on his bike by a truck. Hit and run."

Moon's hands began to shake.

"They're sayin' it was an accident, but no one believes it for a minute," said Pete.

A fury was boiling in Moon's stomach and flaring red in his eyes. Breathe slowly…

"I'm tellin' you, man, they should've burned down all those factories," Pete said, loud and angry. "Only language some people understand."

Moon remained quiet. One…two…three…four…

"Hey, man," said Pete. "You there?"

"Yeah," said Moon.

"Your parents home?"

"No." Five...six...seven...

"You want me to come over?"

"No."

"You sure you're okay?"

"Yeah." Eight...nine...ten...

"I gotta go. It's late. We'll talk tomorrow."

Moon turned off the telephone and the tape recorder and sat for a while in the silent room. He removed the tape from the recorder, brought it down to his room, and placed it in his desk drawer. Then he sat at his desk and began to tap a rhythm on its surface with his hands. He played rudiments and patterns and flams. Right right left left right right left left...right left right right...left right left left...flamadiddle paradiddle...

Was that someone at his door? He got up and opened the door and saw his parents in the hallway. They were in dinner clothes.

Moon and his parents looked at one another a moment.

"I see you know what happened," said his father.

"Pete called me," said Moon.

"It's horrible," his mother said. Her eyes were red, her face was pale.

"Did they really kill him?" asked Moon.

"Our people in Washington are investigating it," said his father.

"We were up on the third floor together," said Moon. "I made a tape recording of him playing my bongos."

"You did?" said his father, looking surprised.

"I liked him," said Moon.

Moon saw his parents glance at each other.

"Oh, you poor dear," said his mother.

"We had no idea at all those people would do something that extreme," said his father.

Moon's heart pounded and his skin burned. He stepped back into his room, closing the door. The poster of the Beatles flapped briefly.

The telephone rang twice, and stopped. A moment later someone tapped on his door again.

It was his mother. "Dear, I keep reminding you, if you keep your door closed, we can't communicate with you. Your English teacher is on the phone."

Moon left the door open and went over to the desk and lifted the receiver. "Hello," he said.

Moon's English teacher, Mrs. Woolsten, said, "Morgan, the essay you handed in about your meeting with Ashraf is very good. You wrote that you made a tape recording of him playing the bongos. Is that right?"

"Yeah," said Moon.

"Please bring it with you next Monday."

"Bring the recording to school?"

"Will you do that?"

"Sure," Moon heard himself say.

"And will you bring your drums?"

"My drums?"

"There will be a memorial service for Ashraf."

"Well, yeah, sure, I'll bring my drums," Moon said.

He sat for a while at the desk, then went downstairs and asked if he could borrow his father's tape recorder. Back in his room, he duplicated the tape of Ashraf playing the bongos.

The following Monday morning, he and his father loaded the drums into the car. Moon sat in the back while his parents rode in front, his father behind the wheel. It was a cold, windy day, the sky ice blue. They said nothing to one another during the trip to the school.

Pete met them in the parking lot and helped Moon carry his drums into the auditorium and set them up on the stage near the podium.

Later that morning, the entire school filed silently into the auditorium. From the dark right wing of the stage emerged Dr. Whatley, followed by the mayor, Moon's parents, and Moon. They sat down in chairs on the stage. Dr. Whatley stepped up to the podium and said that they had assembled to honor the memory of the brave boy named Ashraf who had spoken in their school some weeks before and been killed in a recent accident in Pakistan. He talked about how some people left behind records of their lives—books and music, works of art, deeds. He said that Ashraf had decided to live a life of deeds on behalf of young people his age. He announced that a special school fund would be set up in his memory.

Moon sat in his chair on the stage, listening.

The mayor spoke; then Moon's parents. Then, at a nod from Dr. Whatley, Moon went over to his drums and sat down.

A moment passed, and then over the public address system came the sound of the bongos being played by Ashraf.

Moon waited a minute or two and then began to play an accompaniment to the bongos inside the spaces of Ashraf's beat, a one e and a two e and a three e. His Hi-Hat played the ands, and the snare did two and four, and he added ghost notes to the snare, to make it dance, and then added the bell and slipped into the Seattle sound, *doom-do'ak-doom-d'doom-ak*, and the bongos went *dum dat, dum dat, dum dat*, in that strange rhythm, and then Moon took the drums higher in volume and then was taking them higher still, his sticks beating a frenzied cadence, a rhythm of scalding outrage, and he was thumping, driving, throbbing, tearing through his instruments, pouring onto the world a solid waterfall of sound, and he felt the outrage in his arms and shoulders and heart and the sublime sensation of secret power deep in the very darkest part of his innermost soul.

The bongos fell silent. With a crashing flurry, Moon climaxed the drumming, washed in sweat, strands of his blue-dyed hair clinging to his face and neck. He sat with his head bowed, breathing hard and feeling an exhilaration that he knew would be too quickly gone.

A void followed, a gap in time, and utter silence from the audience. Moon, slowly raising his head, saw his parents staring at him, their faces like suddenly illumined globes. Over the public address system came the hollow hissing sound that signaled the end of the recording of Ashraf playing the bongos.

Nava

THE RED-TILED roofs of the school buildings shone in the spring sunlight. On the grassy field, the players dashed back and forth. The final game of the season. Our side was losing.

Tim Boynton made his way along the row in the bleachers where I was sitting with my classmates and wedged himself into the narrow space next to me. "Hi, Nava, howyadoin'?" he said, as if we'd been friends for years. The fact was, the first time he'd asked me out on a date was about two weeks before, and I'd turned him down. He was seventeen, completing his third year, tall, skinny, said to be smart and well-behaved in class but nasty outside, with dark eyes, acne on his pallid face, and patches of dark stubble on his chin. He wore a scruffy gray sweatshirt and tight blue jeans and had his baseball cap on backward over his straight brown hair.

"I'm fine," I said.

He had an annoying habit of leaning close as he talked. "I just got my hands on half a pound. You want an ounce? Half an ounce?"

I looked out at the soccer field. Students from both schools sat in the bleachers. Parents were present, and alumni, teachers, administrators, the headmasters. It was astounding to me that Tim Boynton was dealing so openly.

Our side scored. The cheerleaders leaped to their feet; the crowd roared. I heard Tim Boynton say, "You're old enough now to start."

I thought of jumping up, circling behind the field, going over to Mom and Dad, who were sitting with friends in another section of the bleachers, and telling them about Tim Boynton. But that wasn't the way students did things in our school; we dealt with such matters among ourselves.

I edged away from him.

"If you change your mind, anytime," he said, eyeing my friends, who were making a point of not looking at him. He grinned at me, stood up, and sauntered away.

A roar rose from the crowd, mixed with moans and cries of "Oh, no!" The visiting team had scored again. We lost that game.

About the time my breasts began to grow and my menstrual blood to flow, a story began to dominate my life. I knew and was properly enthralled by those childhood tales about winged fairies, monsters, kings, princes, and helpless maidens; but the story I remembered with the sharpest clarity was a real-life one that involved my dad.

Dad's story was about the time before he became my dad. In school one day, a teacher got to talking about the war in Vietnam, and it occurred to me to ask Dad if he'd been in that war. He said yes, he was there for close to a year, as a major with Special Forces. He stated matter-of-factly, with no sign of hesitation, that he was wounded and evacuated. He would say nothing more.

Over the years, in response to my frequent questions, he would add to the story. He told me that his unit was ordered forward one day to meet an expected Vietcong attack. The battalion to which he was attached was advancing carefully through a rubber plantation, when it was ambushed by the Vietcong. The firefight, which lasted about ninety seconds, wiped out most of the battalion. Six rounds from an AK-47 struck Dad above his hips, and he lost consciousness. A Special Forces sergeant picked him up and slung him over his shoulder and carried him twenty-two miles back to base camp and the helicopters. The way he carried him, with the wounds pressed against his shoulder, stanched the flow of blood. The sergeant, it turned out, was a Native American, a Navaho.

Dad was close to six feet tall, and solid, the muscles of his stomach like a slab of wood. When he flexed his arms, it was as if hills were suddenly rising. His face was lean and craggy, and he wore his long sandy hair in a ponytail. He wasn't especially handsome. He had calm blue eyes and a somber, self-composed, soldierly manner. He said he'd weighed around one hundred seventy pounds in Vietnam.

"The Indian must've been very strong," I said, the first time I heard the larger version of that story. I think I was eleven years old.

"He still is," said Dad.

"What's his name?"

"Well, I call him Tse Bitai, meaning 'Rock with Wings.'"

"Is that his real name?"

"The name on his army file was Joe Redhill."

"Would you really have bled to death if he hadn't carried you over his shoulder that way?"

"Absolutely," said Dad.

"And I wouldn't've been born."

"That's right, soldier."

Sometimes I'd dream about Joe Redhill lifting Dad to his shoulder and carrying him those twenty-two miles, and even though in Dad's story the firefight had ended, in my dream I'd still hear the automatic-rifle fire and the men shouting, and I'd wake trembling, with my heart hammering and my face wet with sweat.

One night, after drinking a little too much beer, Dad said something strange. He said that when he was hit, his soul flew out of him. He said he felt it leave his body, and then he lost consciousness. When he woke on the hospital ship and the nurse told him what had happened, he lay very still, remembering that his soul had left him and wondering how long one could live without a soul. And then he felt a new soul enter him. It slid into him right there in the bed, feeling cold at first and moving about slowly inside, trying to make itself comfortable, and then growing warm and still. Dad said he had no idea whose soul it was. But he maintained that he was a different man from that day on.

"How were you different?" I asked.

"Well, for one thing, I found I couldn't hunt anymore," he said. "All the old feeling was out of it. I felt really sad about that."

"What were you like before?" I asked.

He said he didn't want to talk about that; he said his new life was born out of that war, and he wouldn't dwell on what he'd been before.

Another time, he told me that after he left the service, he traveled around a lot: California, New Mexico, Arizona, Wyoming; lived along the Columbia River for a while, on a river island with heron, beaver, and white-tail deer. He couldn't stay too long in one place. For some time, he stopped saying that he'd served in Vietnam: people had actually spat in his face whenever he told them that.

His new soul kept urging him on. He ended up finding the Navaho who'd saved his life and who, four days later, lost half his left leg to a land mine.

The Navaho, Dad discovered, lived on a reservation. While there, Dad began to take an interest in Navaho healing, in their chants, prayers, dreams, sand paintings, in the way they tried to control evil. The first time Dad added to his story the part about Navaho healing, I asked him what "evil" meant. He said that Navahos looked at the world as a harmonious creation, and anything that broke that harmony was evil.

"They believe that evil can destroy their society. So they have ways of controlling it."

"What ways, Dad?"

"Soldier, wait'll you put on some more years, and I'll tell you." I was twelve.

From then on, whenever Dad went away to spend time with the Navahos or absentmindedly began to scratch his scars or sank into one of his moods after drinking too much beer, I tried to consider him in the framework of that story. I'd say to myself: He's with the man who saved his life; I'd never have been born if not for that Navaho. Or I'd say: Dad's scars must be bothering him today. Or I'd look at him slumped in his chair, his mouth slack and his eyes staring at nothing, and I'd think: Maybe he's remembering the day he woke up on that hospital ship and realized his soul was gone. His eyes then must've also seen nothing—because what can you really see if you have no soul? Had he been very scared, lying there and thinking about not having a soul, more scared even than when he'd been wounded? I didn't understand what a soul was, exactly, just as I didn't know what evil meant, but I was sure I'd find out about them one day. Anyway, by the time I reached fourteen, that's how I was seeing Dad: through his story about Vietnam and the Navaho who'd saved his life.

We lived in a three-story house that was more than a hundred years old. Dad's study was on the second floor, at the end of the hallway. A Navaho fringed rug, brown-toned and of intricate design, lay on his floor; a magazine rack with periodicals, for which Dad often wrote, stood near his easy chair: *Native Peoples, Warpath, Indian Voice*. Two of the walls were lined with bookcases; the others were covered with academic degrees—Dad taught anthropology at the University of Pennsylvania—and photographs of Navaho healers. One was a picture of Joe Redhill: a lean man, taller than Dad, with long, loose jet-black hair, a rawboned, expressionless face, and dark glittering eyes. He was standing on both his legs, looking very relaxed; Dad had once explained to me that the lower half of his left leg was a prosthesis. Near the photograph hung a framed, glass-covered sand painting—not a picture, but an actual painting—called *Whirling Logs*, created by Dad's Navaho friend out of cornmeal, crushed charcoal and rocks, and sand. It showed two bars intersecting in the center of the painting and forming a cross. Along each arm of the cross was a figure, Father Sky and Mother Earth. Just below the upper left-hand corner of the painting was the head of another figure; the body stretched all the way down to the lower left-hand corner and then on to the lower right-hand corner, and it curved and ran up to the upper right-hand corner, where its legs appeared. Dad said the figure was the Rainbow. He said a completed sand painting was alive, it was holy, like the Cross for Christians and the Torah for Jews. "They use sand paintings and chants in their healing ceremonies," he told me soon after I reached thirteen and he thought I might be able to understand. "Remember, I said they believe that everything fits together in harmony. A person who becomes sick has fallen out of that harmony. The harmony and beauty of a sand painting have the power to heal. So they'll have the sick person sit inside the painting, and they'll do chants and rituals, and sometimes they'll pour the sand on the sick parts of the body so the person will soak up its beauty. Then they'll destroy the painting and bury it, so the sickness won't bring evil to others. Are you following this, soldier?"

Looking at the sand and crushed rocks in the picture on his wall, I asked Dad what was holding it all in place. He said it had all been glued to a board by his Navaho friend, who had it framed and then gave it to him and Mom as a gift when he'd become a healer.

The week I turned fourteen, I asked Dad again what sort of person he'd been when he had his previous soul. We were all sitting at the kitchen table, having supper.

He gave me a sad, dark-eyed look. "You'll need a few more years on you, soldier, before we get to that."

"Were you a troublemaker?"

"Was he ever!" said Mom, her smile bleak.

Mom wasn't pretty, I have to admit. She had dark almond eyes and high cheekbones and olive-colored skin and long, very black hair, which she wore pulled back from her forehead by a red bandeau. In her profession she dealt with neglected and abused children, drug addicts, alcoholics, the families of felons. Her stories were respected confidences, and she never related them to me.

"No more than most my age in Napa Valley," said Dad, with a look at Mom.

"Did you ever use a knife against anyone?"

That jarred Mom a little. "What a thing to ask!" But Dad said, his tone even, "Well, that gets a little complicated. Let's wait for those few more years."

"Did you see in the newspaper two weeks ago about the two fourteen-year-old girls who killed their friend?" I asked.

"The ones in Poland," said Mom.

"And today there's a story about two girls in France. One twelve, the other thirteen."

"I read it," said Dad.

"They killed themselves."

Dad studied me closely and after a moment asked, in his constrained way, "What's up, soldier?"

I gazed down at the food on my plate.

"Is something bothering you, honey?" Mom said. "You don't seem yourself."

"There's this boy in school."

"What boy?" said Mom.

I looked at them. "He's trying to get me to do drugs."

Mom and Dad looked at each other and placed their knives and forks on their plates.

"He came over to me today, said I was old enough to try."

"Just tell him no," said Mom.

"What's he selling?" Dad asked.

"Pot. Maybe he has other stuff. I don't know."

"You won't give us his name, right?" said Dad.

"I can't do that," I said.

"Just tell him no, that's all," Mom reiterated.

"That's what I told him. I told him no."

"Good for you, soldier," said Dad.

"He's come over to me twice this week. The first time was at the soccer game last Saturday. Today I told him if he bothered me again I'd ask you to get your Navaho friend to do his chant against evil."

Dad closed and opened his eyes slowly and asked, "Whatever made you say that?"

"He scared me a little and I got angry and needed to say something."

"Your mom is right. Stay away from him."

"He asked me was I threatening him."

"What'd you say?"

"I didn't say anything. I walked away."

"You did the right thing," said Mom, in her coldest voice. "If he comes over to you again, just walk away from him."

"And don't say anything about Navaho chants or spells," said Dad.

"I'm glad school is over this week," I said.

* * *

Dad left for the Navaho reservation a few days after he handed in his university grade sheets, and he was still gone when I returned from camp in the last week of August. Mom told me he was with his Navaho friend in Washington, D.C., talking to government people about matters involving the reservation. I asked if his friend would be visiting us, seeing Washington was only a hundred miles away. Dad's friend had to fly back home from Washington, she said.

Dad came back by train the next day, looking burned from the sun and as though he'd lost ten pounds. He wore jeans and boots and a cowboy hat, and he smelled of sun and sand. He gave Mom a long kiss on her lips, and me a brief hug—he'd turned careful with his hugs the year my breasts began to show. He told us he now had enough material on Navaho cure ceremonies to complete his third book. "How's Joe Redhill?" Mom asked. Joe Redhill was fine, said Dad. Sends his best regards, sorry he couldn't see us, sudden emergency on the reservation, having to do with ghost sickness and crazy violence.

He handed Mom a small packet wrapped in blue paper, and me a large heavy flat parcel covered in brown paper and tied with twine. Mom's packet contained a silver bracelet, and mine—when I got the string and paper off it—a sand painting. Both had been made by Joe Redhill.

"He said to tell you happy birthday, soldier."

"That's a beautiful painting," said Mom. Dad had placed it on the kitchen table. It measured about two feet by three feet. We all stood there looking at it.

"It's called *Emergence,* from the Blessing Way chant," Dad said.

"It's one of the most beautiful of Joe's I've ever seen," said Mom.

"He said he worked a month gluing it down," said Dad.

"Where are you going to put it?" Mom asked me.

"On a wall in my room," I said.

"Maybe put it in the living room, where we can all enjoy it?" said Mom.

I said nothing.

"Well, it's your painting," said Dad.

"You know Joe Redhill?" I asked Mom.

"Longer than your dad does," said Mom. "I was a social worker on that reservation when your dad got there."

"You met Dad on the reservation?"

"It's a long story," said Dad.

"You want me to have more years before I can hear it."

"You got that right, soldier," said Dad.

"And you want me to have more years before I get to see the reservation."

"Otherwise all you'll see will be a big stretch of hot, dry land and a lot of sick and drunken Indians."

"Can I have Joe Redhill's address? I want to write and thank him."

I carried the sand painting up to my room. Removing the picture of Tom Cruise from the wall near my bed, I stowed it in my closet. Then, standing on the bed, I lifted the sand painting carefully. Though it had been brought all the way from the Navaho reservation to Washington, and then to our house, I worried that the sand might come sliding downward under the glass. I hung the painting on the wall and stepped off the bed. The wall was directly across from the windows, and the painting glowed in the sunlight: a red-bordered light-brown square set inside a long pink vertical rectangle. Nearly touching the top and bottom corners of the square were small vertical gray-and-white rectangles. In the center of the square lay dark-brown, white, and pink circles, from which figures seemed to be rising. Elliptical pink, white, and brown forms hovered outside the red walls of the square.

I gazed at the sand painting. Red and pink and white and brown colors. Whirls and ellipses. *Emergence.*

The third day of school, Tim Boynton slid into the empty chair next to me in the student cafeteria, placed his tray on the table, and put his face close to mine. He wore a creased white shirt and pale blue jeans and a baseball cap. His neck was long and thin, the Adam's apple prominent. Most of the acne was gone from his face.

"Hi, Nava, howyadoin'?"

My friends at the table rolled their eyes, looked away.

"Have a good summer?"

I told him yes. He asked where I'd been. I said a camp in the Berkshires. He said he was with his parents in their summer home on a lakeshore in Maine. "Boating, partying," he added, with a grin. He leaned closer. "New school year, got brand-new stuff." His voice was raspy, and he gave off a kind of high, tense energy.

"Actually…" I said.

"Yeah?"

"Actually, I was saving this seat for someone."

His lips tightened; his face turned red. He reached for his tray, stood up, and walked away.

A week later, he came over to me again, as I was getting my copy of *Macbeth* from my locker.

"Howyadoin'?" he said. "One of my friends wants to know what the name Nava means."

I walked away from him. The next day, he slipped into the seat beside me in the auditorium, where the Drama Society was holding auditions for the autumn performance of *Macbeth*.

"You trying out for this?" he asked.

I nodded.

"Me, too. You sticking around after you read?"

"No."

He brought his face close to mine. "I've got some bones for ya, if ya want. Free. I rolled them myself."

I got up and moved to another seat.

About thirty students sat scattered in the first three rows. Seated at a small table on the stage were Mr. Jacobs, who taught theater arts, and two English teachers. I read for the roles of Lady Macbeth and Lady Macduff. On my way out of the auditorium, I decided to wait in the shadows in the rear and listen to Tim Boynton's audition. As far as I knew, he had never before shown any interest in the school's theater program. He read clumsily.

I heard Mr. Jacobs say, "Thank you."

Tim Boynton said, "That's all?"

Mr. Jacobs said, "We'll let you know."

Tim Boynton nearly tripped as he went down the side steps of the stage. He hurried along the aisle, avoiding the glances directed at him. Coming upon me in the darkened rear of the auditorium, he looked startled and then embarrassed. He rushed out the door, leaving in his wake a slipstream of humiliation.

I was given the part of Lady Macbeth; Tim Boynton was not cast. For the next two weeks, he did not come near me.

Seated in my room at home, memorizing the words of Lady Macbeth, I heard a voice coming from Dad's study at the end of the hallway. I listened for a moment: a man was chanting a strange melody.

I walked down the hallway, the voice growing louder, and knocked on the study door. I heard Dad say, "Come in." The voice washed over me as I opened the door. It was coming from the tape deck on the shelf behind Dad's desk.

Dad looked up from the papers on the desk. "Hi, soldier. Is this too loud?"

"What is it?"

He reached over and turned it off. "Joe Redhill chanting the Moving Up Way, against ghosts. My publisher wants to put a CD of some Navaho chants into the book. Got these in the mail today. There's another one on the tape, of Joe Redhill chanting the Enemy Way, against infection by aliens. They're from a group of chants called the Evil Way."

"What do the words mean?"

"Of the Evil Way? Well, they're asking the sky powers, like lightning and the stars, to protect the sick person. I'll turn it down if it's too loud for you."

"You can play it loud, Dad. I don't mind."

"Are you okay, soldier? You don't look so good. You're not getting sick, are you?"

"I'm okay, Dad."

Back inside my room, I sat over *Macbeth*, memorizing. Joe

Redhill's chanting rose and fell, droning on, like the roll of ocean waves. Repetitious, monotonous, hypnotic. I thought I heard a stirring in the room, a scratching somewhere along the wall where the painting hung, a sound of sand sliding across a hard surface. I turned: the painting was intact. Joe Redhill's chanting moved distinctly through the hallway.

On occasion Tim Boynton would drift into the auditorium during the rehearsals of *Macbeth*. He'd sit in the back and would be gone by the time rehearsals were over. It was early November then. The last of the leaves lay on the ground. I heard them under my shoes one night as I left the auditorium and started along the path to the road that led to the school gate and the street. A car came up behind me, and I stepped to the side of the road to let it go by. It drew alongside me and stopped.

"Hi, howyadoin'?" said Tim Boynton through the rolled-down window.

I turned and started quickly back to the school.

"Hey, wait a minute, wait a minute, just one minute. Can't I just say one thing? I've been waiting for nearly an hour here to ask you just one thing."

I stopped and looked at him.

"Can I ask you one question? Just one question. My friends, they want to know where you got your name."

"I got my name the same way you got yours. From my parents."

"They want to know what it means."

"It's from the word 'Navaho.'"

"Navaho? You mean Nava without the 'ho'?"

"That's right."

"What does your family have to do with the Navahos?"

"Tim Boynton, I want you to stop bothering me."

"Can I ask you one more question? Just one. That's all. I promise."

"What?"

"Why'd you say no when I asked you to go out with me?"

"I don't go out with guys who do drugs."

I saw him staring at me. His face looked bloodless in the glow of the security floodlights. "Okay, we won't do drugs."

"No."

"I promise, no drugs. A movie, burgers and ice cream or whatever, a drive along the river. No drugs."

"I want you to stop bothering me."

He sat behind the wheel, looking at me. "And what'll you do if I don't, Nava-without-the-ho? What'll you do? Snitch? Or ask one of your Navahos to put a hex on me?"

"Tim Boynton, leave me alone!" I suddenly heard myself shout, and I felt immediately frightened by the outburst.

He must've put his foot down to the floor. The car leaped forward, its wheels screeching. I smelled rubber burning. He raced along the school road and shot through the stop sign and on to the street. I walked quickly home.

The next day, I began asking classmates about Tim Boynton. His father was a judge on the Commonwealth Court of Appeals; his mother, a partner in a big law firm in the city. He had an older brother and sister, both in Ivy League universities. He lived with his parents in Penn Valley, in a new stone house with tall windows and cathedral ceilings, an interior pool, and landscaped gardens and trees. Most of the students I talked to knew that he was a dealer. One said that she thought he did it for the feeling of control it gave him over others; he certainly didn't need the money. Another said that, outside school, he hung around with some pretty rough guys.

He came over to me at the water fountain on the second floor. "I hear you're asking about me."

I took a few more swallows before turning to him.

"I don't like it when people ask about me," he said, making a fist of his right hand and raising it to my face.

"What're you going to do?" I said. "Snitch?"

I felt his eyes on my back as I walked away.

Dad made a copy of Joe Redhill's Enemy Way chant and gave it to me. "You like it—it's yours," he said, handing me the tape.

Enemy Way. One of the Evil Way chants. Purge infection caused by an alien presence.

"Is that boy still bothering you?"

"Uh-huh."

"Pot?"

"That's what he's offering me. But I hear he's got other stuff, too."

"Maybe you should give up his name, soldier."

"I can't do that, Dad."

He glanced at Mom. We were in the family room, off the kitchen.

"I don't want that boy to hurt you," Mom said.

"What will it take for you to give up his name?" asked Dad.

"Did you ever give up names?" I said.

They both looked at me, Mom and Dad.

"Thanks for the tape, Dad."

"Sure," Dad said.

I took to carrying the tape to school and back, listening to it on my portable cassette player. The evenings arrived early now. The weather turned cold. A daylong rain washed away the last of the leaves. I'd walk home alone in darkness after our *Macbeth* rehearsals, listening to the chant of Joe Redhill.

In the third week of November, about an hour after the start of the school day, Tim Boynton was called into the office of the headmaster and asked to open his locker. School policy permitted the headmaster to search anything situated on school property for drugs; parents signed a waiver of rights to that effect at the beginning of the academic year. By the start of the *Macbeth* rehearsal that day, everyone knew that the headmaster had found nearly half a pound of marijuana in Tim Boynton's locker. The police were notified, and he was taken from the school in handcuffs. His parents were called; he was suspended.

Mom and Dad heard about it. "Any idea who called it in?" asked Dad.

"It wasn't me," I said.

"I heard it was the drop-in counselor," said Mom.

I didn't say anything.

"Tim Boynton," Mom said. "Isn't his father a judge?"

"Big judge," said Dad.

"Will Tim Boynton go to jail?" I asked.

"No," said Mom. "He'll likely get community work."

"You mean he'll be back in school?"

"Sure," said Mom.

"Was he the one bothering you?" asked Dad.

I nodded.

"Stay far away from him," said Mom.

Tim Boynton returned to school the first day after the Thanksgiving weekend. He showed up at the *Macbeth* rehearsal, wearing a black leather jacket and blue jeans and hiking boots. I could make him out in the rear of the auditorium as he paced slowly back and forth, his head angled one way, his shoulders another. I asked one of the students to accompany me home.

I said to Mom and Dad over breakfast the next morning, "I had this dream last night. Joe Redhill was carrying me."

"What do you mean, carrying you?" said Dad.

"Over his shoulder," I said.

"Why was he carrying you?" asked Mom.

"I don't know. He was carrying me and running. It was really a spooky dream."

"Has that boy been bothering you again?" asked Dad.

"He showed up at the rehearsal last night, but he didn't come near me."

"Well, if he comes near you again, if he says anything to you, I want you to tell us," said Mom.

Dad knocked on the door to my room later that night and

stepped inside, leaving the door open behind him.

"Listen, soldier. Just in case this boy tries something, let me show you a few things you can do." He was standing near the door, looking gloomy. "I talked this over with your mom, and she thinks it's not a good idea. But you never know."

He took a few steps into the room and stood between me and the bed. On the wall behind him was the sand painting. I saw him raise his hands and bring them forward. "Some of these are very painful, others are deadly force," he said. "No one can advise you which to use when. That's your decision. Give me your right hand."

He began the strangest dance I'd ever seen, nothing like they show you in the movies—gliding movements of his legs and sudden swoops and strikes of his arms—all the time talking in a low monotone, guiding me in miming him: how to bend a finger back; how to reach in with a hand on someone's crotch and twist; how to cup the hands and slam them together on the ear, breaking the eardrums; how to use the fist to strike the throat; how to bring the hand against the nose and up; how to bring the side of one's hand against the Adam's apple; how to drive the open hand under the sternum. And never kick, he said, never kick; if they catch hold of your feet, you're done for, finished.

We worked together for over an hour, part of the time using a beach ball. When we were finished, huge drops of sweat were rolling along my forehead into my eyes and down my face and back and quivering arms and legs, and I was certain the exertion had affected my vision, because the sand painting on the wall seemed to be shimmering, its circles and ellipses whirling, the walls of its rectangle and square blurring, its figures dancing—and as a shiver of dread darted through me, I steadied myself against my desk.

"Soldier, this stuff isn't anything you use unless you absolutely have to," said Dad. "We'll go through it again a few more times this week." He was breathing evenly and paying no attention to the sweat pouring down his face. "Much better to know it and not need it than to need it and not know it." He paused. "That boy, he has to touch you, he has to put a hand on you first. Understood?"

I nodded. My throat felt dry and tight.

Dad gave me a long, somber look and then turned and went from the room, closing the door.

I took a shower and climbed into bed. I lay awake, seeing reruns in my head of Dad's balletic motions. Finally, I slept, and I dreamed of Joe Redhill bending over bowls of colored sand and crushed stones, making my sand painting.

Days passed, and Tim Boynton did not come near me. I asked around and was told that he was no longer selling pot. We had one week of rehearsals left until the play. I'd walk home alone. I'd walk with my ears attached to the chanting of Joe Redhill: chants that sounded something like *Ya Ha He Ya Ha Na He*; chants of words, some of which, Dad said, meant: "Black flint, with your five-fingered shield moving around, With this keep fear from me, Keep the fearful thing away from me." As I walked, my ears would be listening to the chant and my mouth would be speaking the words of Lady Macbeth: "O proper stuff! This is the very painting of your fear. This is the air-drawn dagger which you said/Led you to Duncan." And:

"You have displaced the mirth, broke the good meeting/With most admired disorder...."

That's why I didn't see them.

Through the earphones I heard, "Hi, howyadoin'?"

He was standing near a rhododendron bush, in the shadow cast by a streetlamp. Next to him stood a boy I did not recognize.

I stopped and looked up and down the street. The lamp-post lights flickered coldly on the deserted sidewalks. No traffic. Trees black against the moonlit sky.

I shivered and turned. Two figures emerged from a narrow driveway and stood behind me.

"This is Nava," I heard Tim Boynton say.

"Yeah?" said the figure standing next to him. "Nava-without-the-ho?"

"That's right," said Tim Boynton. "Nava the snitch."

"No, I didn't," I said.

"You know how much you cost me?" he said.

"How much you cost *us*," the one next to him said.

"My dad took my car away," said Tim Boynton. "I have to take the bus to school."

I told myself I could make a run for it; my house was only half a block away. I told myself I could scream; surely someone would hear me. I told myself if they hurt me they'd certainly be caught. It made no sense; even Tim Boynton's father's being a judge wouldn't get him out of the mess he'd be in if they hurt me.

"What're we gonna do about you?" Tim Boynton said.

"You're going to get out of my way and let me go home," I said.

"Wow, this babe is real sassy," said the one beside him. He wore a leather jacket and blue jeans and a baseball cap. His voice was deep and nasal.

I told myself they only wanted to scare me. My feet were cold; I could feel my heart beating. They'll go away, I told myself.

"Look, Nava-without-the-ho," said the boy next to Tim Boynton. "My friend Tim here wants to go back into business. We're here to make sure you keep your mouth closed."

"I'm not a snitch," I said. "I just want him to leave me alone."

"Well, now, we don't have no control over Tim's private life. You know what I mean? We're in business with him and we got to protect our investment."

"Someone else snitched, not me," I said.

"Yeah? Who?"

"I don't know. All I want is for him to stop bothering me."

"Hey, Tim, can you stop bothering this sassy kid?"

"I'll bother her all I want," said Tim Boynton sullenly.

"There," said the boy. "What'll you do if he bothers you again?"

"Why are we standing here talking?" said one of those behind me.

"Stay cool, man," said the one next to Tim. "And if he won't leave you alone, Miss Nava-without-the-ho? What then?"

I felt my heart pounding and a dryness in my mouth.

"Hey, talk to me, Nava-without-the-ho."

"What is this, a goddamn meeting?" said the one behind

me. From the sound of his voice I could tell he had stepped closer.

"Don't you touch me," I said.

"No?" he said.

"Hey, what've you got there?" the boy standing next to Tim Boynton said suddenly.

I stood very still.

He came up to me. "What're you listening to?"

"I'm not listening to anything," I said, trembling.

He reached up and pulled the earphones from my head. The wire went taut, held by the cassette player in the pocket of my jacket. He reached into the pocket and removed the player.

"Hey, Jack," said Tim Boynton.

"A little payment for what she cost us," said the boy.

"We agreed—"

I stood there looking at the cassette player in the boy's hand. "Give me the tape back," I said.

"What?" said the boy.

"Could I have the tape back?"

"Hey, guys. She wants the tape back."

"Please," I said.

"You're lucky we don't shove it up your—"

"Jack," Tim Boynton said. "You told me there wouldn't be any—"

"Shut your mouth," the boy said to Tim Boynton. "Just shut your dumb mouth."

"That tape is very important to me," I said.

"Yeah?" said the boy. "In that case, you can have it."

He removed the tape from the player and waved it in front

of me. I reached out for it and he laughed and drew it back. Then he brought it forward and pushed its edge sharply into my breast.

"It's all yours, Nava-without-the-ho," he said.

I reached for it, my blood hammering. I had my fingers on it. He pulled it from my hand and slipped it into a pocket of his leather jacket.

From behind me I heard someone laugh.

There was a brief silence.

I remember staring at the pocket into which the tape had vanished and feeling it had been ingested by some loathsome spirit. I imagined it being swallowed, washed into a pit of bubbling acid, where it would swiftly dissolve. Amplified waves of sound surged through the street—my voice returning to me as echoes of my shouted words: *"Give me back that tape!"* I heard the boy's hiss: "Shut your mouth, bitch!"; heard Tim Boynton's urgent "C'mon, let's go." I knew that Dad could make another copy of the tape; but all I saw was *that tape* curling and melting—and then a sudden image of the four of them breaking down the door to my room and bursting inside and jumping on my bed and reaching up to remove Joe Redhill's sand painting from my wall. I knew that they intended to smash the painting, scatter the living square and the rectangles, the emerging figures, the spirals and circles. And so I moved, a sudden thrust and a twist, and the boy let out a scream. Tim Boynton tried to step out of my way and stumbled backward into the rhododendron. I began to turn, but someone behind me put an arm around my neck. I used my elbow, heard an intake of breath, got my hand on a finger and bent it back and heard a howl, and then I felt the air rushing out from deep inside me and I fell to the street, sure that my soul had just left my body. Then a distant shout and lights and the sounds of scurrying feet and suddenly someone picking me up and running.

I think losing your soul is when you can't tell a story about something that has happened to you.

Mom said that the doctor told her my voice would return, the damage to the vocal cords would heal, but not for a while. Someone else would have to play my part in *Macbeth*. Mom said to keep writing down what happened, to keep trying to make a story out of it. Mom said the version I'd written was not yet a story, I needed to write a story that began with the first time Tim Boynton tried to sell me that stuff until what happened on the street.

When I first woke, Dad told me that a man in a passing car had seen the fight, found my name and address in my copy of *Macbeth*, and carried me to the house. Dad said that it was a police matter now and I had to give up the names of whoever did it, and I wrote down "Tim Boynton and someone called Jack and two others." Dad shook his head and said, "Four goons on one girl." The next day, Dad said that Tim Boynton had been picked up by the police and had told them the names of the others. Dad said the one called Jack was found with the tape of Joe Redhill's chant still in his jacket pocket, and with a bruise where I got to him. "Outstanding," Dad said. Mom grimaced.

I was back from the hospital and in my own room. The sand painting hung on the wall near my bed. Dad had made a tape of Joe Redhill doing a Holy Way chant that restored health.

"Well," Mom said, after reading my third version. "That's for sure a real-life story."

"I guess I have those years now," I wrote.

"Yes, might be you do," said Dad quietly.

"And things'll be all different for me, too," I wrote.

Never before or since have I seen a greater sadness than I saw in my dad at that moment.

Isabel

WHEN FOURTEEN-YEAR-OLD Isabel lost her father and her little brother, she crossed into a world enormous with emptiness and gray-lit with grief. Days came and went—endless and vacant; nights—black, cold, stark. In the early mornings she heard her mother crying. Darkness in Isabel's head and ice in her heart; her body weighty as stones, her clothes rubbing like sackcloth. Frequently her heart jumped as she heard her father talking or singing and her brother riding his tricycle in the driveway.

After three months there was disquiet among relatives and friends, murmurs of concern: "Isn't it time Isabel put an end to her grieving?" "These *moods* of hers!"

"Isabel, you're not eating, you're not sleeping, you're going to make yourself very sick," her mother warned one day, speaking not only to her daughter but also to herself, for she was unable to dispel the police and newspaper and television accounts of torn metal and flesh that lodged in every corner of her mind. She was by then desperately fearful of raising her daughter alone.

"Mom, I *hear* them. They can come back," said Isabel.

Her mother shivered with dread. "What is the *matter* with you? Stop acting this way!"

Isabel did not respond, for, at just that moment, she was certain she had heard her father enter the house and call out in his tenor voice, "I'm home, everybody!"

Months with a therapist did little to dispel Isabel's certainty that her father and little brother were still alive in some nearby invisible realm and could be returned to full life if only she could find out how. Gradually growing wise to what lay behind the queries of her therapist, she told him one day that she was no longer hearing or seeing her father and brother. Vastly relieved, her mother terminated the therapy. Two days later Isabel heard her father singing an aria from his favorite opera, *Tosca,* while her little brother was jumping up and down on his bed.

Eight months after the deaths of her husband and son, Isabel's mother met Charles Magruder in the Museum of Art, at the opening of the Jasper Johns retrospective, in front of a painting in which the forms depended entirely upon how one focused one's eyes. Charles Magruder made some remark about the tricks the eyes sometimes play, and Isabel's mother said something about the tricks that life plays. One comment led to another, and they soon discovered their similar situations—his wife had died a year before, and he had a fifteen-year-old daughter.

In the weeks that followed, they saw each other often; in the spring, they thought it might be time for their daughters to meet.

Isabel tried to keep her face from showing any emotion when she saw the new diamond ring on her mother's finger and learned that her mother's new friend and his daughter would be coming to dinner that Sunday. About both she'd been told very little, her mother saying she preferred that Isabel see them through her own eyes.

When the doorbell rang the Sunday of the dinner, Isabel reluctantly accompanied her mother to the front door and set eyes for the first time on Charles Magruder and his daughter.

She saw a tall, handsome, smiling man in his mid-forties, lithe, tanned, with thick brown hair, deep-set blue eyes, and a square chin. He wore an oversized white shirt and black-and-white checked trousers. On the sleeves, collar, and button front of the shirt, which hung loose over the waistband of his trousers, were colored reproductions of paintings by Vermeer, Rembrandt, and van Gogh.

"Hello, hello," he said, and held out to Isabel's mother the bouquet of flowers he carried.

"Charles, you look like a harlequin by Picasso!" said Isabel's mother with a high laugh.

Isabel saw her mother's girlish fluster and the color rising on her normally pale features, and was suddenly aware of how the daisy-embroidered gray tunic and gray pants and navy-blue tee-shirt she had on left her looking a good deal younger than her forty years. She was a lovely woman, with long dark hair, brown eyes, high cheekbones, and full, fleshy lips. Thickish ankles were her one physical flaw; to conceal them she favored pants or boots. Taking the flowers, she opened the door wide, and Betsy and her father stepped across the threshold into the center hall.

"You like it?" asked Betsy's father, smiling delightedly and running his hands over the front of his shirt. "Believe it or not,

I got it from a flower catalogue. Hello, this must be Isabel." He had a slightly nasal baritone voice. "I've been looking forward to meeting you."

"Hello," Isabel said.

He extended an enormous hand, ridged with tendons and veins and sparsely covered with pale-brown hair; the hand swallowed Isabel's palm and fingers.

"This is Betsy," he said.

"Hi," said Betsy, handing Isabel a small package wrapped in purple paper and tied with a green ribbon.

"Thanks," Isabel said.

"They're quartz earrings, rose-colored, set in sterling silver," Betsy said.

"Honey, the idea is to let people open the gift and see for themselves," said her father.

"I hope you like them," Betsy said. Her voice was husky, and she blinked as she spoke. She had small lips, a long face, and large gray eyes, and she wore no makeup. She was taller than Isabel, her shoulder-length dark hair cut in a pageboy style. The loose-waisted light-purple dress she wore concealed her very slender body and flat chest.

"Isabel will love them," said her mother. "You can open it later, dear. Why don't we go inside and make ourselves comfortable."

They entered the carpeted living room, which overlooked a stone patio and a sweeping rear lawn bordered by a stand of birch and maples. Squirrels scampered in the recently cut grass and a solitary cardinal dropped suddenly from the sky, lingered regally for a moment on the low wall of the patio, and flew off: a flash of scarlet in the early-evening light.

Isabel's mother brought drinks—Scotch on ice for Betsy's father, a glass of white wine for herself, diet sodas for the girls—and invited them all to help themselves to the raw vegetables and guacamole. She sat down beside Betsy's father on the white corner couch and gazed eagerly at the two girls.

Isabel and Betsy had taken the two black easy chairs that stood at a ninety-degree angle to the couch. Betsy sat tensely perched on the edge of her chair. She looks a little like a grasshopper, Isabel thought. Or a hungry bird.

"Well, here we are, finally." Betsy's father smiled at Isabel. The smile wrinkled the corners of his eyes.

Isabel sat very still, saying nothing.

Betsy's father said genially, "Your mom and I, we know that we have a big head start in the getting-to-know-each-other department, but we're sure you and Betsy will catch up and become good friends."

He smiles too much, Isabel thought.

"Do you have anything you want to ask me?"

Isabel did not respond.

"Go ahead, anything at all," he prompted, with an engaging smile.

Isabel had many questions: Why are you here? What makes you think you can take the place of my real father? How am I supposed to live in the same house with a strange man and his daughter *and* my father and brother? She asked, "What do you do?"

"What do I do?" Betsy's father echoed, with a glance of surprise at Isabel's mother.

"Why, I told you, dear," said Isabel's mother. "Charles is an architect."

"But you didn't tell me what he builds," Isabel said.

Out of the corner of her eye, she saw Betsy looking at her, blinking.

"You mean what do I design," said Betsy's father.

"Yes, what do you design?"

"Well, let's see. I've designed country homes, shopping centers, art galleries, museums, a private home in Society Hill, an office tower in Minneapolis, a public library in downtown Chicago, and the new amusement park near Seattle. I got a big kick designing the spook house there."

Isabel said, "You designed a spook house?"

"That's right."

"How do you design a spook house?"

Her mother crossed her legs and sat back, absently rotating her engagement ring and letting herself relax a little. Betsy, who seemed to have lost interest in the conversation, was looking around the room—at the red-brick fireplace; at the stone Aztec heads and the small wood sculptures of Alaskan seals and African warriors on the mantel; at the abstract paintings on the cream-white walls; at the gleaming black upright piano and the occasional lamps. Her eyes blinked repeatedly.

Betsy's father ran a hand over his thick hair and took a sip of Scotch. "That interests you, does it? Well, now, let's see. If you have a house that's already standing, you fill it with surprises—like loud noises, dancing skeletons, ghoulish laughter, monsters leaping at you across doorways, things of that sort. If you start with nothing, then what you need is a concept, a story. You could build a house and put all kinds of things into it, as long as they fit the story."

"I don't like spook houses," Betsy said suddenly.

"I know you don't, pet," her father said.

"My dad once took me and Bobbie to a spook house," said Isabel. "Bobbie got very scared."

"I told your father it wasn't a good idea," said Isabel's mother.

"Who's Bobbie?" asked Betsy.

"My little brother," said Isabel.

"Oh, right," said Betsy, blinking.

"Did your dad tell you that I own an art gallery?" said Isabel's mother to Betsy.

"Yes, he told me," Betsy said.

"We exhibit paintings and sculpture, and sell to private collectors, museums, and corporations. Do you have a favorite artist?"

"I don't know anything about art," said Betsy.

"Hey, pet, don't knock yourself down like that," her father said. "Didn't you tell me and your mom that you liked Degas?"

"I don't anymore," said Betsy.

Her father put down his empty glass. His face looked flushed beneath the tan.

"I think," said Isabel's mother after a brief moment, "it's getting on to dinnertime."

She had prepared a dinner of green salad, poached salmon with wild rice and snow peas with red peppers, and lemon ices. During the salad course, Betsy's father said to Isabel, "Your mom told me you have a leading part in your school play."

Isabel, feeling Betsy's eyes on her, did not respond.

"Which part is it?" asked Betsy's father.

"I play Laura in *The Glass Menagerie*," Isabel said.

"Laura! Well, it's hard to imagine someone as pretty as you playing someone as plain as that," Betsy's father said.

"Last year, Isabel was Emily in *Our Town*," said her mother.

Betsy and her father helped clear the dishes, and Isabel and her mother brought the next course to the table. As they sat eating the poached salmon, Isabel's mother said to Betsy, "Your father and I want to build new lives after the terrible tragedies we've been through."

Betsy sat bent forward over her plate, chewing slowly, her dark hair concealing most of her features.

"There's no point at all to shutting down one's life," Betsy's father said to Isabel. "Everybody gets to have only one time around, and the clock doesn't stop for anyone."

Isabel was trying to keep her face frozen hard.

Later, as they were eating the lemon ices, Betsy's father said to Isabel, "Your mom and I have years ahead of us, and we want to live them together."

"We're hoping to get married this summer," said Isabel's mother.

Isabel and Betsy looked at their parents and then at each other. Betsy's face reddened. Isabel felt a stab of fear.

"Your father would not have wanted me to spend the rest of my life alone," said Isabel's mother.

"Nor would your mother have wanted that for me," said Betsy's father.

"Why don't you girls go upstairs for a while and get better acquainted," Isabel's mother said.

"That's a good idea," said Betsy's father. "I'll help clean up."

Betsy followed Isabel up the carpeted staircase to the second-floor hallway. Isabel opened the door to her room, and

Betsy stepped inside and closed the door. She stood looking around the room.

The bed was covered with a flower-patterned yellow spread. The papers on the desk, the volumes in the bookcase, the framed photographs on the dresser—all tidy, orderly. Light-yellow stippled walls and thick, tufted orange carpeting. On the wall across from the windows, a poster showing pink ballet slippers; nearby, a black-and-white reproduction of an Escher etching of fish metamorphosing into birds; on the adjacent wall, a color poster of Meryl Streep. On the third wall, against which stood the desk, hung a large framed photograph of a tall man standing next to a young dark-eyed boy; in the background was the fieldstone front of the house. The furniture in the room, of pale wood, glowed warmly in the light of the ceiling fixture. Yellow lace curtains covered the windows, which looked out on the grassy back lawn and the woods.

"Everything is so neat," Betsy said.

"My dad taught me to be neat," said Isabel.

"Was that your dad and brother?" Betsy asked, pointing to the photograph.

Isabel lowered her head and nodded.

"My mom died of breast cancer," Betsy said. "She was sick for three years."

"My dad and brother were killed in a crash. The police said the van that hit them was going very fast."

"What did your dad do?"

"He was a doctor. What about your mom, what did she do?"

"She made jewelry."

"Did she make the earrings you brought me?"

"No," Betsy said. "I wouldn't give away any of the things my mom made, not even to my best friend."

Isabel hoped her face wasn't showing the heat she felt rising inside her.

"I like your dress," Betsy said. "I wouldn't wear it, I'm too skinny. But it looks nice on you." She gazed intently at Isabel. "You know, you're very pretty. And you have nice hips and breasts."

Isabel, not knowing how to respond, remained silent.

"I barely have breasts at all," Betsy said, placing both hands on the lower part of her chest and pushing up. "You see? Nothing. Maybe I won't die of breast cancer."

"Why do you think you'll die of breast cancer?"

"I heard my aunt say it's inherited."

Isabel felt a sudden shiver of dread.

"You know, your mom is very pretty," said Betsy. "My dad likes her a lot."

Isabel thought she had to respond to that, so she said, "When they get married, we'll be half-sisters."

"No we won't," said Betsy. "We'll be stepsisters."

"Oh, that's right," Isabel said. "Stepsisters."

"There's a big difference," Betsy said.

Isabel and Betsy saw each other again two weeks later, in a dimly lit restaurant across the Delaware River from the Camden aquarium. They sat at a table near a huge window that faced the river and the Benjamin Franklin Bridge. The towering girders seemed insubstantial in the soft light of the setting sun.

"Charles, we should order," said Isabel's mother. "The waiter is coming back for the third time."

"Right," said Betsy's father, finishing his drink and signaling for another.

Isabel's mother laughed lightly. "I mean food," she said.

Betsy, who had been gazing out at the bridge, saw her father's reflection in the window and turned to him. "Daddy," she said in a half-whispered voice.

"What?" said her father.

"Daddy, please."

"I'm not driving, pet, so where's the harm?"

Isabel's mother smiled brightly. "This is a celebration dinner, Betsy dear. There's nothing wrong with a drink or two at a celebration."

"That's right," said Betsy's father. The candle in the hurricane lamp on their table shone with a flickering glow on his striped dark suit and lemon-yellow shirt and crimson tie.

"Darlings, we have the caterer, the minister, and the wedding date," said Isabel's mother.

"I'm a very happy man," Betsy's father said. "I don't mind telling the whole world how happy I am." His eyes were moist. "I hope we'll all be happy."

"We'll be happy, Daddy," said Betsy. Isabel nodded and looked away.

"You're both dear girls," said Isabel's mother, dabbing at her eyes.

"They're going to be like sisters," said Betsy's father, the high color on his face visible even in the candlelight.

After dinner Isabel's mother drove them to the apartment house where Betsy and her father lived. In the car, Betsy's father, who was a little drunk, said to Isabel, "Show you what we're giving up because I love your mom."

The high-rise took up an entire street on the Benjamin Franklin Parkway. They walked through an enormous marbled and mirrored entrance hall and stepped into a paneled elevator. When they emerged on the fourteenth floor, Isabel saw her mother smiling and leaning into Betsy's father as he took her arm.

Entering the apartment, Betsy's father switched on a tall halogen lamp near the door. He left the light subdued and led them through a large living room to floor-to-ceiling sliding glass doors, which opened onto a brick terrace. The low houses of the city lay before them, and off to the left rose the new towers, bathed in blue and green lights. It was a clear night, the sky lit by a quarter moon; stars were emerging. Isabel saw the illumined Parthenon-like Museum of Art and the dark flow of the river. From the expressway rose waves of traffic noise. To the south along the rim of the city were the storage tanks and flaming stacks of the oil refineries and the blinking wing lights of arriving and departing airliners.

"Hard to let this apartment go," Betsy's father said. "I designed the interior myself. Built only two bedrooms, so not enough space here for both you young ladies."

"We know you'll want your privacy," said Isabel's mother.

Betsy's father gazed at the city and took a deep breath. "I never get tired of this view," he said. "Rhoda loved this view."

"It's making me dizzy," said Isabel.

"Betsy, why don't you show Isabel the apartment," said her father. "Show her what we're giving up for life in the suburbs." He smiled at Isabel's mother and put his arm around her waist. "Helen, I'm going to enjoy redesigning the house," he said, and kissed her on the cheek.

The living room was furnished with black leather easy chairs and end tables of glass and brass. A maple table, a buffet, and sharp-edged chairs filled the dining area. The pine floor reflected warmly the subdued halogen light. Against one of the walls stood a maple bookcase filled with volumes on architecture. Walking with Betsy, Isabel saw, through an open door at the far end of the hallway, a room with a four-poster double bed and a green-and-beige floor runner with a geometric pattern.

"That's my dad's room," said Betsy.

The door to Betsy's room was open. Isabel followed Betsy inside and was immediately struck by the colors: light-purple walls and deep-purple curtains and two yellow chairs, a red desk and a purple dresser and bed. On the walls—posters of Tom Cruise, Madonna, Alanis Morissette, Whitney Houston, James Dean. On the bed—faded blue jeans, black panty hose, a black brassiere, a gray sweatshirt. A scattering of schoolbooks and CDs on the desk. A purple bookcase crammed with Harlequin novels. Amid the clutter on the top of the dresser stood a framed color photograph of a middle-aged woman: long-faced, alabaster-skinned, with shoulder-length dark hair cut in pageboy fashion and half-moons under her eyes.

Isabel stood looking around the room.

"That's my mom in the picture on the dresser," Betsy said.

"My mom would never let me paint my walls this color," Isabel said.

"Well, it's my room," Betsy said. "My mom let me choose the colors I like." She turned to Isabel. "Can I ask you something?"

Isabel looked at Betsy's pale face and small mouth. She's not pretty at all, she thought.

"Something personal," Betsy said.

Isabel nodded hesitantly.

"What was your dad like?"

Isabel was quiet a moment. Then she said in a low voice, "My dad was, mostly, sort of easygoing. He liked telling us funny stories." As she talked, she heard her father's laughter in the hallway outside Betsy's room. "He saved people's lives. He was always reading medical journals, and he liked listening to opera. Sometimes he and my mom would shout at each other, but they loved each other a lot. Sundays we'd all go out for long walks or on picnics or to Longwood Gardens or the zoo. He made great salads and pasta. What was your mom like?"

"My mom had this great sense of humor and liked everyone and always said whatever came into her head. She wasn't, well, she wasn't all that good-looking, but everyone liked her. She and my dad, they fought a lot, mostly about his drinking. But I think they were really in love. Can I tell you something?"

"What?"

"Your hair, it's so long and beautiful. Did your dad have red hair?"

"My dad's hair was blond," Isabel said.

"Can I touch it?" Betsy asked, and without waiting for a reply, put her hand on the hair alongside Isabel's forehead. Isabel felt Betsy's fingers lightly stroking her hair and saw a strange look enter her eyes: they appeared to grow enormous, translucent, the color of watery gray ink. She ran her tongue over her lips, drew her upper lip back, and caught her lower lip between her teeth.

"It's like silk," Betsy said.

Isabel stepped back. "Please don't," she said.

Betsy lowered her hand. "My hair feels like rope," she said.

"It looks pretty."

"It's stringy and dry and ugly," Betsy said.

"It's not ugly."

"Isabel, you don't have to say things to make me feel better."

Isabel felt her face burning.

"When my mom died and people were saying all those things—'She's at peace now, dear' and 'May you be spared further grief, dear' and 'Your mom's no longer suffering, dear'—I swore to myself I'd never say dumb things like that, I'd say what I felt, and if anyone asked me how I felt about my mother dying, I'd say I felt like shit. But you know something? No one asked me."

"I'm sorry," Isabel murmured.

"It's okay, it's okay," Betsy said. "We got that cleared up. What I wanted to say was that your mom has nice skin and nice hair and a really cool, sexy figure. And she and my dad have slept together."

Isabel stood absolutely still, staring at Betsy.

"In my dad's bedroom. They thought I was asleep."

"I don't think I want to hear about it," Isabel said after a moment.

"Do you have a problem with me telling you that?" Betsy asked.

"I just don't want to know about it," Isabel said.

Betsy gave her a severe look. "I thought you'd want me to share everything with you, since we're going to be one family."

Isabel felt little shivers of nausea.

During the ride home, the car cruising along the nearly empty West River Drive, Isabel said, "Mom, last night I heard Daddy again."

"Oh, dear. I thought we were done with that, Isabel."

"He came into my room and said you mustn't get married."

"You cannot keep doing that, darling."

"I heard him, he was so real."

"It really upsets me to hear you talking this way. Do you want to see Dr. Kaplan again?"

"Mom?"

"What, dear?"

"Betsy told me you and her dad slept together."

"Oh, my," said her mother.

"Did you?"

"I warned Charles we should be more discreet."

"Mom?"

"This is the only time I will talk to you about my very private life, young lady. Yes, I've slept with Charles. I love him. You can't begin to imagine how starved I was for sex with someone I loved. Should I be telling you this? Anyway, I've told you. I'm very happy and proud that Charles loves me. I need a husband, and you need a father."

Isabel heard the thundering of her heart. She couldn't think of what to say, and thought, His smile has you fooled.

"Yesterday I saw Bobbie on our back lawn," she said. "He was running after squirrels."

"Isabel, stop it!"

"I saw him."

"You're going to make yourself sick."

"Mom—"

"You're going to make *both* of us sick!" She was rigid with anger. "I want you to *stop* it!"

Isabel stared out the car at the lighted boathouses on the opposite shore. Lamppost lights reflected like stilettos in the black mirror-smooth surface of the river.

"We'll always remember Daddy and Bobbie in our hearts," she heard her mother say. "It's time for us to get on with our lives. We've grieved enough."

During the weeks before the wedding, the den was redone, its new look open, spare, sharp-edged, contemporary. In the living and dining rooms, new, modernist furniture supplanted the old. Many of the knickknacks on the fireplace mantel were replaced by small models of the structures designed by Betsy's father, including a miniature of the spook house near Seattle: a strangely asymmetrical gray three-story building, with odd-size doors and windows and a winged gargoyle poised on the peak of its slanting roof. Some walls were moved; in others spaces were cut for new doors and windows. Ceramic floor tiles, a Corian countertop, and natural-wood cabinets were installed in the kitchen, along with new appliances. Isabel's father's books and journals were sent off to a medical school library; Charles's architecture books now crowded the shelves in the den. One day while Isabel was in school, men came with a truck and emptied Bobbie's room of its furniture; later that same day, its walls were scraped in preparation for a new coat of paint.

The one room untouched by the renovations was Isabel's; she retreated to it often. There she read, did her homework, listened to music, stared at the photograph of her father and little brother, lay on her bed with her hand over her eyes, or stood at her window, gazing out at the back lawn and the flower beds and the squirrels and the family of cardinals that seemed to be favoring the patio that year.

Charles appeared frequently at the house to confer with the contractor and builders. He wore all kinds of flamboyant clothing—jackets and shirts and trousers and shoes garnered from exotic catalogues—and his eyes shone as he walked about the house with Isabel's mother or sat with her on the patio, always with a drink in his hand. Often Isabel heard their laughter; at times it startled her as it echoed through the downstairs rooms. One day she happened upon them in the den, embracing and kissing, Charles's large hands clutching tightly her mother's buttocks, pressing her into him. Isabel stepped unseen from the room, her legs shivery, her heart thundering. Some days later, she went past the open door of their soon-to-be bedroom and saw the freshly painted cream-white ceiling, the newly installed recessed light fixtures, the maple walls and cabinets, the shag carpet and window drapes, the new four-poster king-sized bed. She burst into tears and fled to her room.

Once, Charles brought Betsy with him. The two girls went up to Bobbie's old room, now freshly painted in purple. Betsy stood in the vacant room, looking around, her eyes glistening. "I can't wait to move in," she said.

The days went by. Isabel felt herself a frightened dweller in the space that had once been her home.

Isabel's mother and Betsy's father were married that summer in a large white tent on the back lawn of the house. Isabel's mother looked stunning in a long white dress of raw silk and French lace that followed the contours of her lovely form and concealed her ankles, and Betsy's father stood tall and handsome in a glistening white suit, white shoes, a brocaded white shirt, and a red silk tie. The minister, a man in his fifties, spoke about the bride and groom as people who were repairing the injured order of the world. Betsy's father placed the ring on Isabel's mother's finger, and Isabel and Betsy heard them pronounced man and wife. Betsy's father kissed Isabel's mother for what seemed a long time. Isabel saw Betsy turn away.

Some of the guests were relatives and friends; most were strangers to Isabel. She hovered along the perimeter of the reception, listening to people talk—"Isn't it wonderful how they found each other!" and "What a good-looking couple they make!" and "Wasn't the wedding service lovely!"—and wondered where Betsy had gone to; she was nowhere to be seen. After a while Isabel edged toward the woods. From the dappled shadows came the sweet sounds of her father singing the aria about stars from *Tosca*. She saw him clearly through the trees, tall, blond-haired, carrying Bobbie on his shoulders. *Daddy*! she called, running toward them. *Bobbie*! she cried. Her father walked deeper into the woods, singing. He moved so quickly, singing, and Bobbie swaying on his shoulders, and she could not keep up, and soon the singing faded, and she came to a halt on mossy earth and heard only the hum of winged insects gliding through the greenish air. She returned to the lawn.

The sun was bright, the air hot; the light broke upon the grass like shards in her eyes. She saw her mother and Charles, arm in arm, moving among the guests, saw the flash of her mother's wedding ring, and heard Charles telling people how happy he was. He held a champagne glass in one hand and seemed to be leaning heavily on Isabel's mother with the other. Betsy suddenly appeared at Isabel's side. "My dad is drinking too much," she said. Isabel said, "He's celebrating." Betsy said, "Look at him," and stomped off. By the end of the afternoon, he was drunk. Isabel's mother, a patient smile on her face, helped him into the car. To the shouts and whistles of farewell from the guests, they left for the elegant Center City hotel where they were to spend their wedding night.

The guests began to leave. The caterer's crew removed the remaining food, the dishes and silverware, the tables and chairs, and drove away. The slanting golden light of late afternoon moved imperceptibly across the lawn and the house.

Inside her room Isabel had changed out of her silk print gown into jeans and a tee-shirt, when she heard a muffled crash from the adjacent room and Betsy's voice through the wall, raised in anger. Isabel hurried out of her room and along the hallway. Betsy's door was wide open.

The men who had moved Betsy and her father into the house had deposited her cartons in neat rows along the walls of her room. The neatness had been shattered. The room was an astounding clutter of clothes, jackets, sneakers, shoes, toppled stacks of CDs and books, brassieres, panty hose.

A large suitcase lay open on Betsy's bed.

"I'm trying to pack for the bike trip, and I don't know where anything is," Betsy said, standing over a carton. She had changed to jeans and a tee-shirt and was in her bare feet. Her hair was in disarray, her hands fluttered helplessly.

"Didn't you make a list?" asked Isabel.

"I can't find it."

"What's all this here?" Isabel pointed to the clothes and shoes spilling from the open cartons.

"I need special clothes for the bike trip and I can't remember where I packed them."

"Well, let's look," said Isabel.

They cleared a space in the center of the room, searched the cartons on the floor, then arranged them against the wall. It took more than an hour before they found the clothes and shoes Betsy needed for the bicycle club trip she was flying out to join the next day.

"Thanks," Betsy said. "I wouldn't've found it by myself."

"Sure," said Isabel. She sat on a carton, watching Betsy pack.

Outside, it was dark. Through Betsy's open windows came the sounds of a light wind in the maples along the street.

"You know something?" Betsy said abruptly. "I can finish up later. I'm starved."

They went downstairs, found chicken and potato salad and sodas in the refrigerator, and sat on bar stools at the island in the kitchen. Betsy started to tell Isabel about the itinerary of her four-week bicycle trip along the coast of Maine. Isabel listened and then described the theater arts camp near Tanglewood where she would spend July while their parents were on a honeymoon cruise. Then they talked about Isabel's school, which Betsy would enter that fall: classes, teachers, sports, cliques, drugs, boys. "I don't do drugs, and I don't like boys," Betsy said. Isabel said boys were okay, but sometimes they didn't know what to do with their hands.

"What do you suppose my mom and your dad are doing right now?" Isabel suddenly asked.

Betsy fixed her with an amused look. "Probably you-know-whating, if my dad isn't too drunk."

There was a moment of silence as Isabel stared at Betsy. Then the two girls burst into laughter.

"You've got a piece of chicken on your chin," said Betsy. She leaned forward and removed it.

"Thanks," said Isabel.

They sat at the table, eating and glancing at each other from time to time.

"Can you see your mom sometimes?" Isabel suddenly asked.

Betsy's eyes blinked and then narrowed. "You mean *now*?"

"Can you hear her?"

"My mom is dead," said Betsy.

"I see and hear my dad and Bobbie."

"No, you don't," said Betsy.

"I saw them in the woods after the ceremony."

"No, you didn't," said Betsy.

"My dad was carrying Bobbie on his shoulders."

"Your dad is dead," said Betsy.

"He was singing."

"And your brother is dead," said Betsy.

"Still—there's maybe—"

"And buried," said Betsy.

Isabel sat staring at Betsy. She felt her frozen heart and then the slow opening of a fissure and suddenly from her widening heart a gulping sob and from her eyes an overflowing pool of tears. She wept awhile, her shoulders shaking. Betsy sat in silence and then went to the pantry and returned with a box of tissues.

"Come to my room for a minute," said Betsy.

Upstairs, Betsy went to one of her cartons, from which she removed a small leather case. Opening the case, she showed its contents to Isabel.

"My mom made these. She gave them to me before she died."

Isabel saw a cluster of exquisite necklaces, miniature flower pins in silver and gold, rings bordered by tiny gems and bearing stones in intricate geometric designs.

"Aren't they beautiful?" said Betsy. She reached into the case and drew out a ring with a floral design into which was set a gleaming red stone. "I want you to have this," she said.

"Oh, no," Isabel said.

"I want you to," said Betsy. "It's my thanks for helping me tonight."

"I didn't do anything," said Isabel.

"Put it on," said Betsy. "Let's see if it fits."

"I really didn't—"

Betsy reached over, took Isabel's left hand, and slipped the ring onto the third finger.

"A perfect fit," said Betsy, smiling.

Isabel felt the ring on her finger. "It's beautiful," she said.

"I won't mind sharing my mom's jewelry with you," said Betsy.

"Thanks," said Isabel. Her heart was beating strangely.

"You want to know something?"

"What?"

"I think Isabel is a really beautiful name."

"It was my dad's mother's name."

"I hate my name. But…Isabel. *Is*-a-bel. *Eas*-a-bel. Your name sounds like music."

Isabel's face felt suddenly hot. She said, "I've got to pack, too. I'd better say good night."

"Do you really like the ring? Because if you don't, you can have any one you want."

"I love it. I really do."

"Okay," Betsy said. "Good night, then."

"Good night," said Isabel.

Inside her room, Isabel packed very quickly, showered, and climbed into bed. She tried to read for a while, then switched off the lamp and lay quietly, listening to the house. In the darkness, she touched the ring Betsy had given her: warm and tight on her finger. How silent the house was, not a sound from the walls or the wind. She tried to think what her mother and Betsy's father were doing, and just then thought she heard a soft tapping at her door. Startled, her heart fluttering, she lay still. Probably squirrels, their spooky scratchings often heard throughout the house. But the tapping came again, louder this time.

Isabel switched on the reading lamp and slipped from the bed. She crossed the room barefooted and opened the door.

In the doorway stood Betsy. She had on a nightgown, pale purple in the dim light of the hallway. Isabel saw her eyes: enormous. They covered, it seemed, half her face.

"Isabel," Betsy said. She glanced at the ring on Isabel's finger. Her lips formed a shy smile.

As though in a trance, Isabel thought, Daddy wouldn't've wanted me to be alone, and opened the door wide.

"Is-a-bel," Betsy murmured as she stepped lightly across the threshold.

Max

FOR AS LONG as I can remember, we'd spend Thanksgiving Day with Mamam and Papap. That meant loading up the car the afternoon before and making the four-hour drive through the Pennsylvania hill country to the small town where they lived, with me and Maxie in the back seat and Dad driving and Mom beside him. It was a strange and marvelous ride, to a mysterious forest-filled world, the highway dipping and climbing, and the tall trees following the contours of the hills, and sometimes a dead deer along the side of the road, and the slowly fading light of day, and at the end of the ride, Mamam and Papap. They'd come out of their house to greet us, Papap tall and pink-faced and full of smiles, Mamam smelling of hot bread. And the next day, Thanksgiving Day, with most of the family sitting around the food-heaped table, there would be the stories about farming and the weather and the latest in tractors and the hunting season and the bureaucrats in Harrisburg and the new roofs that had to be put on and the new wells that had to be dug. And the stories about Uncle Max.

Maxwell T. Cooper. Max to everyone. Uncle Max.

It seemed everyone had something to say about Uncle Max. But I paid no attention to their stories, because I had plenty of stories of my own: animal stories, witch stories; stories about my dolls; stories I made up on waking and before going to sleep; all kinds of stories. None of the stories about Uncle Max interested me. To tell the truth, those stories scared me; they seemed to come from a dark region far beyond my warm and lighted room.

During school recess one spring morning when I was in first grade, I was playing near the playground fence when a small airplane appeared about a thousand feet overhead. The playground was crowded with children and teachers. Commuter aircraft always flew over our neighborhood on their approach to the airport; no one paid any attention to them. But that airplane—silver and yellow, twin engines buzzing like some giant mosquito—suddenly banked, came around in a wide circle, and flew over us again.

It did that four or five times.

By then some of the teachers had begun to notice it. One teacher stood gazing up uneasily, craning her head at the blue sky. The airplane flew by again, banked, and came back around.

Right then, out of nowhere, a helicopter appeared, with a terrifying chop-chopping roar that beat against my ears. I saw it come close to the airplane and circle it, slowly. Suddenly banking, it began a sideways slide through the air below the belly of the airplane—and at that moment the teacher put a whistle to her mouth. The piercing metallic sound penetrated the noise of the helicopter and the airplane. Everyone froze. *"Inside!"* I heard the teacher shout. *"Inside! Now! Now!"*

There must have been about seventy or eighty of us in that playground, and we all ran frantically toward the large double doors of the school. One of the kindergarten students tripped and hurt her leg, and I helped her to her feet and half carried her to a teacher at the doors. Just as the last of us made it inside, there was a horrendous crash and a loud explosion. I felt the noise in my legs and on the back of my head, a jarring all up and down my spinal column. The entire school building seemed to move. Doors and windows rattled. Some of the students screamed and began to cry. The teachers hurried us into the classrooms. From the windows I saw pieces of the airplane and the helicopter—a burning tire, a scrap of wing, a tail section, a crazily spinning rotor blade—striking the asphalt surface of the playground and go tumbling against the chain-link fence, and other pieces crashing into the cars parked across the street and onto lawns. Sheets of burning fuel cascaded over the playground. A small piece of metal struck one of the windows and bounced off, cracking it. The teachers ordered us away from the glass panes. I smelled rubber burning and heard people shouting and running along the corridor outside the room. It all seemed to be happening in slow motion, as in a movie. We heard sirens, and soon there were police and firemen everywhere and crowds of people on the street. I was shaking and needed to go to the bathroom, and I slipped out of the room and started down the corridor, which was filled with firemen and police, running back and forth. I went to the bathroom and sat there awhile, and then returned to the classroom. Soon parents began showing up to take their children home. I was still shaking a little and wondering where my mom was; I thought it was taking her a long time to get there. At last, she came rushing into the classroom and scooped me up and held me to her a long moment and then carried me out of the school's back doors. The air reeked with the smells of burning rubber and fuel and hot asphalt. Mom held me tight as she carried me through the crowds, and I asked her to put me down.

Still shivering, I asked her what had happened. She said she'd heard about it over the radio: the small airplane's landing gear seemed to have jammed, and the helicopter pilot circled to see if it had come down all the way, and the rotor blades had sucked the airplane into the helicopter.

"You poor darling," Mom said. "Thank God you're all right and no one in the school was hurt."

We were walking through the streets of the neighborhood. "Are the pilots dead?" I asked through chattering teeth.

They'd both been killed, Mom said, along with a passenger on the airplane.

Then this question suddenly rose from someplace inside me: "Was that how Uncle Max got killed?"

She looked at me in surprise.

"All that noise and everything?"

"I don't know."

"And that fire?"

"Maybe you should ask your dad," Mom said.

I asked Dad about it when he came home from his office later that day. He'd heard about the accident. A United States senator was the passenger who'd been killed. Dad was a big man, and he held me very close. He said, "You don't want to talk about that, pumpkin. You're only six years old."

"Six-year-olds know amazing things these days," said Mom.

"Yeah? Well, I don't think we need to add my brother to our daughter's amazements right now," Dad said.

I said, "Daddy, just before the crash, the teacher who blew her whistle and told us to go inside...she's Vietnamese."

Dad looked at me but didn't say anything.

"My teacher said she came here when she was about ten years old."

Dad didn't seem to know how to respond to that.

"My teacher said she saved a lot of lives today. Did Uncle Max save lives in Vietnam?"

Mom's face stiffened.

"That's not what he was sent there for," Dad said.

We lived at that time in a semi-detached gray stucco house along an asphalt road and across from a patch of weed-choked earth that separated us from the railroad tracks on which commuters rode back and forth from distant suburbs to Center City. I remember clacketing trains and the windows of my room rattling as the express from Harrisburg went roaring by, frightening my dolls and stuffed animals, which I always arranged carefully around me in my bed.

One night, shortly after the accident in my school, I had my first dream in which a train left the tracks and went careening across the road onto our lawn, crushing the azaleas and the front porch. The stucco walls of our house fell away like paper; my windows shattered and splashed across my pale-blue carpet; my walls splintered. The entire street side of my room crashed inward as the train came plunging toward me, engine roaring and wheels spinning. The pipes in the walls burst, spraying water over me and my bed and the floor. My animals and dolls lay soaked and crushed around me, and a huge train wheel came to a stop inches from my head. I screamed and screamed, and Dad finally came running into my room, Mom right behind him. I woke with my heart thundering and realized it had all been a dream. Mom held me, but I really wanted Dad. After they left I lay still, waiting to fall back asleep. And just before sliding into sleep, I found myself wondering why it had seemed to me that Mom and Dad had taken such a long time getting to my room. Uncle Max, I thought, would have been there sooner.

The next morning, when I talked with Mom and Dad about the dream, they said it was not unusual to have such a dream after an accident like the one at school. But I could tell they were troubled by what I said about them taking too long to get to my room and about my notion that Uncle Max would have gotten there sooner.

A few months after that accident, and some weeks after Mom became pregnant with Maxie, we moved to a large single house. I'd really loved our old house. Mostly we moved, I think, because the old house wouldn't have a room for my new brother, what with Dad needing a study and Mom an office for their work.

Soon after we'd moved, Mamam and Papap called and said they wanted to come and fix up Maxie's future room. Mom said the room sure needed fixing. Dad told me that Mamam and Papap were great at fixing things. He said that he grew up watching them fix everything from a leaking pipe to a dead furnace, and listening to Mamam read aloud every morning and evening from the Old Testament and the Gospels, and learning from Papap about fishing and hunting. Maybe he and Maxie would go fishing and hunting with Papap one day; Mom and Dad knew that the baby was a boy, and they'd already chosen his name.

Mom shook her head and said that fishing would be okay, but not hunting. Even fishing she wasn't too keen on, she said, adding that the only fishing she really liked was for clients to whom she could sell a house; Mom was in the real estate business.

Dad said that, with all due respect to his beautiful wife, Maxie was his son, too, and he especially wanted him to know about hunting and the use of firearms, because he firmly believed that knowing how to use firearms taught you to appreciate life, and the best place to learn the value of life was in woods and marshes, where you could pull the trigger on a bird or a deer or a bear and see and touch the lifeless body of the creature you'd killed.

I remember Dad's words: "See and touch the lifeless body of the creature you've killed."

Dad said, "Where will Maxie better get to understand that acts have consequences, that some deeds, once done, can never be undone?"

Mom said, "Robert, are you serious, or are you just being a clever lawyer?"

"I'm very serious, Annie," said Dad.

Mom gave him a look that was close to horror and said, "I swear to God, sometimes I don't recognize the man I'm sleeping with." She placed both hands on her swollen belly. "That's your brother Max talking, not you," she said.

Dad didn't like that. His face turned crimson, but he was quiet.

Early spring, Mamam and Papap took the train south to 30th Street Station in Center City, where Dad met them. They were in their middle fifties then, tall and lean, with robust faces and blue eyes and strong hands. I loved them very much, my Mamam and Papap. When they worked in Maxie's room, they wore blue jeans and blue denim shirts. Maroon baseball caps, with the words "Cooperston High School" in white, covered their graying hair; Papap taught biology in that high school.

I remember the second day after they arrived, I stood in the doorway to Maxie's room, watching them work and wanting them to play with me. Mamam said, "No, we can't play now, Emmie. We need to finish your brother's room."

"But, Mamam, let's play the train game," I said.

"What game is that?" asked Papap.

I said, "We climb on the train with my animals and toys and there's a big crash and we all go falling off."

They stopped their work and looked at each other and then at me. "We'll play later, darling," Mamam said. Papap slowly shook his head and lowered his eyes.

In the days that followed, they lifted the old carpeting from the narrow wooden floor strips, rolled it up, and hauled it outside to the trash bins near the garage. They spackled the cracks and holes in the faded green walls and painted the windows and sills a bright creamy yellow. They put up new wallpaper, on which red and yellow and purple fish swam in a pale-blue sea. They scrubbed the oak floor and let it dry; then they covered the floor with new beige carpeting.

Often, as they worked, they'd quietly sing hymns—"A

Mighty Fortress Is Our God" and "How Firm a Foundation" and "A Shelter in the Time of Storm." Mamam had a sweet musical voice; Papap's voice was deep and throaty, like Dad's. Once, as I stood in the doorway, watching them work, Papap asked me to hand him a paintbrush. I brought it to him and we started talking about what I was learning in school, and I told them about my teachers, Mrs. Foster and Mrs. Clayton, and about Rapunzel and the stories of the Sphinx and the Minotaur and that the earth was a huge ball and how Columbus and his men found America and that Spanish soldiers wore helmets and coats of steel and carried swords and guns, while the Indians only had spears and arrows, and I recited by heart "The Owl and the Pussycat" and "Mary, Mary, Quite Contrary." They listened and looked at each other with deep smiles, and Papap murmured, "Smart girl," and Mamam said, "Praise the Lord."

The morning Mamam and Papap were to return home, I saw them go past my room, and I followed and watched them enter Maxie's room and get down on their knees and bow their heads. Papap prayed that Maxie would be born healthy; Mamam recited from the Bible, the Psalm about the Lord being one's light and salvation, and prayed that the Lord would see that they'd had enough sorrow in their lives, and that Mom should have an easy time delivering Maxie.

That night it stormed, and a school bus turned slowly into our small street from the main road, one block away. Our new house was only two blocks from my school, and yellow school buses went up and down the street mornings and afternoons. But never during the night! Now the bus moved carefully along the rain-drenched asphalt, and about fifty feet from our house, it picked up speed. Lying in my bed, I heard the revving of the engine and stepped quickly to the window—in time to see the bus skid from the street and mount the curb, barely missing our sycamore tree. It advanced solemnly, ponderously, as if in slow motion, through our rhododendrons and azaleas and up the front lawn—and, with a terrible sound, crashed into our living-room picture window. The house shook. Stone and glass shattered. I was standing with my face against my bedroom window; the impact broke the panes; they cracked, cascaded. Splinters of wood and shards of glass showered upon me. Rain on my face and arms mixed with sudden wellings of blood. I screamed with pain but this time the scream remained inside the dream and no one rushed into my room. I screamed again—and suddenly a tall man, lean and wiry, sprang from the shadows. It was Uncle Max, in his Special Forces uniform, with green beret and Silver Star, a rifle slung over his shoulder! He plucked me from the debris and held me close to him and in a single leap carried me out of the ruined house—and I woke in my bed, sweating and trembling and staring at the moonlight on the window and, very slowly, shedding the dream. After some while, I got up to go to the bathroom.

The house was quiet. On my way back through the night-lighted hallway, I stepped into Maxie's room. There was the empty crib in the corner. The air was fragrant with new carpeting and fresh paint. Wallpaper fish glided in the bluish moonlight shining through the windows. The room was as soundless and serene as the house, softly gleaming, and waiting.

Maxie was born two weeks early. One morning, while Dad was in Chicago on a business trip, Mom's water broke. Our neighbor drove her to the hospital, and I walked by myself to school. By the time Dad arrived, I was at the hospital, and Mom was awake and holding Maxie to her breast. He was swaddled in a blanket and had on a pointed cap. Dad kissed Mom and looked closely at Maxie.

"Well, what do you think of your new brother?" Dad asked me.

"He looks skinny," I said.

"Just five pounds," said Mom.

"He looks like Max," said Dad.

I peered closely at little Maxie and didn't think he looked at all like the pictures I'd seen of Uncle Max.

"He won't look like anybody if he doesn't get busy and start sucking," said Mom.

Mamam and Papap came down the day after Maxie was born. I was in the hospital room with Mom and Dad when they walked in. They took turns holding Maxie.

"The Lord bless you and keep you," Mamam said in a low, fervent voice to Maxie, who was asleep in her arms. "We thank the Lord for bringing you safely into the world."

"Amen," we all said.

"Well, son," Papap said to Dad. "You got a fine-looking boy here."

Dad smiled proudly.

"How do you feel about your new baby brother?" Mamam asked me.

"Are all babies this small?" I asked.

"Some are, most aren't," Mom said.

"I can't get over how he's the image of Max," Papap said.

Mamam suddenly began to cry and handed Maxie back to

Mom, who was sitting up in her bed. Papap put his arm on Mamam's shoulder and talked to her quietly. Dad was sitting on a chair near Mom; they were both looking at Mamam. Mom motioned to me and I went over to the bed and she handed me Maxie and I stood there holding him.

"He's your new brother," Mom said. "Tell him you love him."

I was seven years old, but I felt as if I was holding a bundle that was only a little heavier than air.

Mom and Maxie were in the hospital for five days, because Maxie's weight dropped to below five pounds and it took two days to bring it up again. When Dad brought them home, Mom went straight to bed.

That same day, the live-in nurse Dad had hired let me go into Maxie's room. He lay asleep in his crib. I didn't think he looked at all like Uncle Max. Well, maybe some similarity about the shape of their mouths. I moved closer to Maxie and stood on tiptoe, looking through the bars of the crib. Very gently, I touched his fingers, so pale and tiny and beautiful. His face was white; almost chalk white, I thought. I reached through the bars of the crib to touch his face, and he woke and began to cry. The nurse ushered me from his room.

The year Maxie was three and I was ten, we'd made the usual plans to be at Mamam and Papap's for Thanksgiving. But Maxie suddenly became sick—something about his eyes—and we couldn't go. I wanted to go alone by train—the high forested hills; and deer on the roads and among the trees; and Mamam's hot bread and turkey and pumpkin pie; and sleeping in Uncle Max's bed in Uncle Max's room; and sometimes a short walk in the forest behind the house with Papap; and all the stories about Uncle Max—but Mom wouldn't hear of it.

The next year, the week before Thanksgiving, Maxie had a lingering cough from a bad episode of bronchitis, his second bout in six months. Dad insisted the country air would be good for Maxie, and when our doctor said that the trip by car couldn't hurt him, Mom said okay but Maxie was not to go running around or playing wild games until the cough was gone.

Maxie was astoundingly good-looking; a miniature of Uncle Max, as I could now see. Pink features, cornflower-blue eyes, flaxen hair. And with the liveliest, most expression-filled face anyone could imagine. Sometimes I'd catch Mom and Dad looking at him in absolute awe. But often enough their gaze was dark with worry. Even at four, Maxie hadn't entirely left off his odd waddling gait; he walked in an awkward ducklike way and often tripped over his feet and bumped into furniture. Mom and Dad really fussed over him, especially when he was sick.

About an hour after we started winding through the hills of central Pennsylvania, it occurred to me that Maxie was no longer coughing. We were driving in heavy rain, and abrupt patches of mist that were like white blankets suddenly dropped over the car and then quickly pulled away. Maxie sat next to me in the back, belted into his junior car seat, playing with his current favorite toy, a plastic Huey helicopter Dad had given him, blades and all, with half a dozen miniature figures of a uniformed pilot and troops inside, which Maxie could snap into place and remove, as he wished. Mom was asleep in the front seat.

We emerged from a sudden tunnel of curling mist and

started into a turn and came upon four cars stopped along the side of the road. Two had collided, and the drivers of the others appeared to have halted to render aid.

A short, balding middle-aged man stood hatless on the side of the road, talking into a cellular phone, while a second man was leaning forward, his head poked into the open window of a car whose front was as wrecked as the trains and buses I used to dream about. He wore a brown lumber jacket, and the rain had darkened the seat of his gray trousers. The man with the phone looked at us as we drove slowly past. I noticed the driver of the second damaged car: a woman, her head on the steering wheel, her face turned toward the road, her eyes wide open.

"Damn, that looked like a bad one," I heard Dad say after a long moment.

Mom stirred and woke and glanced out her side window.

"Did you say something?" she asked.

"Crash back there," said Dad.

"Back where?"

"About a half mile."

"Why didn't you stop?"

"Enough people helping already," said Dad.

"You should've stopped and asked," said Mom.

"Not with the kids," said Dad. His voice had a strange tremor to it.

Mom turned in her seat. "How're you two guys doing back there?"

"We're fine, Mom," I said.

"You okay, big guy?" asked Dad, looking at Maxie in the rearview mirror.

"I didn't maked them crash," said Maxie.

"I didn't *make* them crash," said Dad, looking away from the mirror.

"You should've stopped," said Mom.

"And add to Emma's catalogue of crash dreams?" said Dad.

"I haven't had a crash dream in a long time," I said. I couldn't understand why he hadn't stopped. Uncle Max would've stopped.

"*Now* I maked them crash," said Maxie, and swinging the Huey in an arc over his head, he brought it down against an arm of his car seat, sending the pilot and troops tumbling out.

"Not a toy for a car ride," Mom said to Dad.

"He can't hurt himself with it," Dad said.

Maxie was leaning forward in his seat and waving his arms at the toy soldiers scattered on the floor of the car.

I shook my head. "No," I said.

Maxie started to wail.

"Emma," said Dad to the rearview mirror.

"He'll only do it again, Daddy," I said.

Maxie coughed and took a wheezing breath. His pretty face turned ugly when he cried: small trembling mouth, pink blotches on his cheeks, nose running, eyes red and streaming.

"Emma, please," Mom said.

I released the seat belt and slid down into the narrow valley between the seats and gathered up the plastic soldiers, feeling in my legs the yawing and swaying motions of the car. I climbed back into my seat and popped the soldiers into the Huey, replacing one of them with special care. This one is Uncle Max, I told myself. I thought how wonderful it would've been if someone had been able to do that for Uncle Max when his Huey had gone down: gently pick him up off the ground and return him to an undamaged helicopter. All the pieces suddenly together; no fire; the hot stink of burning rubber and flesh vanished into the air. Then Mamam and Papap wouldn't be so sad in their souls most of the time, and I wouldn't have had those crash dreams, and Uncle Max might even be a general and come home to Thanksgiving dinner in his uniform and service ribbons and wearing his green beret and Silver Star.

I put on my seat belt. Maxie happily swung the Huey over his head. The doctor had said that the way he kept bumping into things, he probably needed glasses. He was going to be tested next week. He coughed again, a dry wheezing cough, and arced the helicopter close to my face. I leaned away from him. I really disliked him at times, even if he was my brother.

We turned off the paved two-lane mountain road onto the narrow dirt road that would take us to another paved road and, very soon afterward, to Mamam and Papap's house. Just then a deer leaped out from the dark woods to our right and came to a halt in the middle of the road. Dad stopped the car in a skid of dirt and pebbles.

In the headlights, the deer, a buck, seemed a gargantuan animal, his skin tawny, his eyes golden lamps. He lowered his antlered head against the car.

I felt my scalp tighten and the backs of my legs go cold. This had happened to us twice before, a buck challenging us for mastery of the road. I was scared and excited. Maxie let out a whimper.

"Will you look at that guy," said Dad quietly.

"He's beautiful," I said.

"That's a ten-pointer," said Dad.

"Uncle Max would shoot him," I said.

"No he wouldn't," said Dad.

"He'd shoot him right between the eyes," I said.

"That's not where you shoot," said Dad.

"What did you say?" asked Mom, turning to me.

"Why wouldn't he?" I said. "He shot the one hanging over the fireplace."

"Buck season doesn't start until the day after tomorrow, that's why," said Dad.

"Oh," I said. "But if it *was* buck season."

"Well, Max would get him, all right," said Dad.

"Will you two please stop," said Mom.

Dad hit the car horn. Maxie, startled, cried out. The buck reared, slowly swinging his head. Dad hit the horn again. Wheeling abruptly, the buck clambered off the road and went crashing back into the woods.

Maxie coughed and wheezed.

Dad started the car moving along the dark road.

"Are there bears here?" I asked.

"Sure are," said Dad.

"Did Uncle Max ever hunt bears?"

Once more, Mom turned in her seat to look at me.

"Good idea to leave bears be," said Dad.

"What *can* you hunt?" I asked.

"Well, let's see if I remember this," said Dad. "October seventh, the archery season starts, and goes for two weeks. October eleventh, you can go after squirrel, grouse, and woodcock. Starting on the last Saturday in October, it's the season for ringneck, rabbit, and turkey, for one month. The day after Thanksgiving, like I told you just before, is the start of the buck season, and that goes on for two weeks. Then there's a two-day doe season, starting December fifteenth. And December twenty-sixth starts a three-week time for archery and muzzle-loading and fifty-caliber rifles, flintlocks, like in colonial times, flash in pan, and ignition."

"There's the house," Mom said, sounding relieved.

"Don't shoot many with those flintlocks, but it's a lot of fun," said Dad. "Max was good with them."

"Strange idea of fun," said Mom.

Dad turned the car into the driveway and stopped before the garage door. "We're here," he said.

The back door opened, and Mamam and Papap came out of the house. I half expected Uncle Max to appear behind them. I heard the loud barking of Papap's hunting dogs—two full-grown German short-haired pointers. The driveway, the house, and the broad sweep of back lawn were lit with yellow floods. The light ended at the dark wall of the forest, which dipped and rose and climbed to a stream and continued up a tall hill and then on for some miles to a lake and to railroad tracks, along which ran the trains to Ohio and Indiana and Illinois and the Great Plains.

Mamam enclosed me in her gentle hug. She smelled of hot baking bread.

"We saw a buck on the dirt road," I said.

"Plenty of them around," said Papap.

"Let me look at you," said Mamam, holding me at arm's length. "My, you've grown."

"Eats for two," said Dad.

"'Children's children are the crown of old men,'" Mamam said. "And also old women." She'd greeted me with those words many times before.

"Let me give you a hand with those bags," said Papap.

"Maxie is stressed out," said Mom. "I'll put him straight into his pajamas. We need to bring in the red bag first."

Dad looked at Maxie and frowned. Mamam and Papap busied themselves helping unload the car.

"Will I sleep in Uncle Max's room again?" I asked.

"Well, it's been your room all the while, dear child," said Mamam. "No reason to be different tonight."

Dad watched as Maxie left the driveway and started alone on the stone walk to the door. He fell, picked himself up, went on a few feet, and then stopped. The barking of the dogs had suddenly turned shrill, frenzied. Maxie ran to Dad, who picked him up.

"Those are Papap's dogs," said Dad. "You remember those dogs, don't you?"

"Sure you remember them," said Papap. "The little puppies you played with."

"They're not puppies anymore," said Dad. "What're they barking at?"

"Don't know," said Papap. "Barking all day. May be a bear or two in the woods."

"Go inside now," said Maxie, sounding ready to cry again.

"You bet," said Dad.

"Is he okay?" asked Papap.

"Looks like he'll be needing glasses," said Dad.

"Maxie?"

"Looks like it."

"Is that right?" said Papap.

The air was cold, mountain cold, sharp and thin, not in the least like the air where we lived. It entered my nostrils; I felt it deep inside my lungs. Deliciously frigid shafts. Tall-mountain-trees-stripped-of-leaves cold. Boughs-reaching-toward-the-iron-winter-sky cold. Fishing-through-a-film-of-frozen-water cold. I loved it. I loved the smell and taste of cold buck-season air.

Mom had gone into the house with Mamam. Maxie clung to Dad. I picked up one of the light bags. The barking of the dogs grew more shrill, echoing in the forest. With Maxie still clinging to him, Dad closed and locked the car. We started up the stone walk to the house.

Mamam and Papap belonged to a singing church that had a Thanksgiving Day service. It was a small white church, at the head of a street in Cooperston that sloped steeply down toward the river, and that day the furnace wasn't putting out enough heat and people sat in their coats. Most of Dad's family lived in and near the town, and they all came in for the service. There were about two hundred people inside. Maxie grew noisy and fidgety during the offering, and Mom had to go outside with him, so she missed hearing Mamam and Papap sing, "Now Thank We All Our God." I always thought it had to be very hard for them to give thanks on the same day that Uncle Max had died in a helicopter crash in Vietnam, Thanksgiving Day, but somehow they managed to do it year after year. They stood there in front of everyone in the church, singing, "Now thank we all our God, With hearts and hands and voices, Who wondrous things hath done, In whom His world rejoices." Then they sang, in memory of Uncle Max, "I Gave My Life for Thee." And then we all sang, "When peace, like a river, Attendeth my way, When sorrows like sea billows roll—Whatever my lot, Thou hast taught me to say: It is well, it is well with my soul."

I noticed Mamam's hands trembling slightly and saw beads of sweat on Papap's face and head—despite the cold air in the church—matting down his thinning gray hair.

Later that day, we all sat around the dining-room table in Mamam and Papap's house. I always worried the table might fall from the weight of all the food on it. There were, if I'm remembering right, fourteen of us: uncles, aunts, nephews, cousins. I listened carefully to all the talk about Uncle Max. Uncle Fred, who was a farmer and didn't like deer—"big mice," he called them—talked about the deer Max bagged the week he'd turned thirteen; old Aunt Ellie, who was very devout and hard of hearing, reminded us that Max had known dozens of church hymns by heart; Mamam said what she said every year: how proud she was that he'd attended Gettysburg Military and then graduated with honors from Penn State at the age of—would you believe it?—eighteen; Cousin Herb, who'd served in Korea with the Seventh Infantry and was a carpenter, told us, in his quavery voice, about Max's nine months in Thailand and eleven months in the jungles of Vietnam, some with a tribe of Montagnards; fat Cousin Andy, who smoked cigars and owned the main hardware store in town, the one near the train station, described how Max had saved a paratrooper from a Roman-candle chute during a battalion jump—he'd gotten that story from Max himself; Dad told how, when he was ten and Max was sixteen, Max had pulled him out of their burning pickup after it was broadsided by a six-wheeler that had jumped a stop sign; and Papap told about taking Max hunting when he was only ten, and the two of them coming upon a bear and her three pups, and he and Max standing silent as trees, Max calm, motionless, not a tremor from him, the bear and her pups passing so close they could see her yellow eyes. That was the day he knew there was something special about Max, Papap said.

At that point Maxie, who'd been coughing and wheezing and making a mess of his food, announced that he needed to go to the bathroom. Mom looked almost happy to be able to leave the table with him and not have to listen to any more tales about Uncle Max. The air in the dining room was very warm. Everyone around the table went on eating and talking. Mamam got up to bring in the pumpkin pie.

I asked Papap if he would take me into the forest the next day and show me about hunting.

"Well, now," he said, giving me a look of surprise.

"Please, Papap," I said.

"Best ask your dad and mom if it's okay," said Papap.

"Daddy?"

"Well, I don't know," Dad said.

"Maybe too much of Max in this room," said Uncle Fred. "Making the girl a little loony."

Mamam came back into the dining room with the pumpkin pie.

"You missed something," said Papap.

"What did I miss?" Mamam asked.

"Emmie here wants to learn hunting," said Cousin Herb.

"Is that right?" Mamam said calmly.

"In this family, girls don't hunt," said Aunt Ellie. Her deafness, we knew, was selective. What she wanted to hear, she heard.

"Papap," I said, "you took Uncle Max out when he was my age."

"Well," said Papap, "that was Max."

"I can learn as fast as Max."

"Well, I don't know."

"I know all the dates by heart."

"What dates are those, honey?"

"All the hunting dates," I said.

"What hunting dates do you mean?"

They were all looking at me.

"October seventh, the archery season starts, and it goes on for two weeks. October eleventh, you can go after squirrel, grouse, and woodcock. The last Saturday in October starts the season for ringneck, rabbit, and turkey, for one month. The day after Thanksgiving is the beginning of the buck season, and that goes on for two weeks. Then, starting December fifteenth, there's a two-day doe season. And on December twenty-sixth starts a three-week time for archery and muzzle-loading and fifty-caliber rifles, and also flintlocks, like in colonial times, flash in pan, and ignition."

They had all stopped eating and were just sitting there looking at me. Dad's eyes were wide, and I saw him shake his head.

"Well," Papap said, blinking. "Where'd you learn all that?"

"I told it to her on the ride here," said Dad.

"Is that right?" said Papap.

"I just told it to her once."

"Well," said Papap. "Isn't that something?"

Mamam passed her hand over her eyes.

Right then Mom came back in with Maxie. She settled Maxie into his chair and sat down next to him. "This pie looks very good," she said to Maxie. "Would you like some?"

Maxie pursed his lips and shook his head.

"You're missing something that's really good. Sure you don't want any?"

"No pie," said Maxie.

"This was Max's favorite pie," said Mamam.

"No pie," said Maxie loudly.

"Okay, okay," Mom said. She looked around the table and smiled wearily.

"Well, it can't hurt just to go for a walk," said Papap.

"Thank you, Papap!" I said.

"A walk where?" asked Mom.

"Just a walk into the forest," said Papap. "Sort of a long walk. Emmie here and her Papap."

Mom looked at Papap and then at me.

"Can't hurt at all," said Mamam.

Mom looked slowly around the table. Everyone was sitting quietly and watching her. Even Aunt Ellie. I could see their eyes going from her to Maxie and back to her.

"Used to take Max on long walks day after Thanksgiving," said Papap. "Some of the best memories I have, those walks."

Mom looked down at the dish of pumpkin pie on the table in front of her. Maxie coughed and sniffled. Mom picked up her fork and began to eat.

It was warm under the down quilt. Smooth sheets, firm pillow. Papap's dogs barking. My eyes, used to the darkness, made out Uncle Max's collection of hunting rifles mounted on the walls. Maybe Papap would let me take the little twenty-gauge Uncle Max had started with. Ask Mamam to ask Mom to let me.

Mamam had kept everything of Uncle Max's, it seemed. Piles of yellowing military magazines in the closet. And the bookcase filled with volumes about soldiering. Pictures of Uncle Max in hunting gear and in uniform and with his graduating class at Gettysburg and at Penn State. No women in the Gettysburg Military Academy graduation picture. I thought I heard a train go by. Sometimes, if the forest was really still and the wind was right, I'd hear the trains on their way to Ohio and Indiana and Illinois and the Great Plains. Here, in this house, I'd never once dreamed a crash. None that I could remember, anyway. My eyes were closed and I was certain that I was asleep, but I opened them and, no, I was still awake. At least I thought I was. In Uncle Max's room, I couldn't always be sure about wakefulness or sleep; the room, crowded with the urgent whispers of his life, often blurred the borders between sleeping and waking. Outside, the dogs were still barking.

It snowed during the night. I woke to a vast exhilarating whiteness. I washed and dressed and went out of the room.

Mamam and Papap were in the kitchen. Mamam was cooking eggs and flapjacks.

"Morning," they both said, in quiet voices.

The house was very still.

"Emmie, you want to dress much warmer than that," said Mamam. "That was a real snow last night."

"I'll take care of it," said Papap.

We sat at the table. Papap recited the blessing over the food.

"Little Maxie woke up during the night," said Mamam.

"Twice," said Papap. "Poor little guy. Bad cough."

"Papap," I said, "can I take Uncle Max's twenty-gauge along?"

He glanced at Mamam and then shook his head. "Maybe not today. Maybe when you get to be thirteen."

"Thirteen? That's a long way, Papap."

"Well, maybe next year. Plenty to do in the meantime to get ready. Try different loads in the range in town tomorrow, for starts, if it's okay with your dad and mom."

"Never be in a hurry for this," said Mamam. "There's two families that depend on us for their winter meat. That's good reason for doing it. But never be in a hurry to take a life."

"Finish up eating," Papap said, "and I'll get you some of Max's kid clothes. We'll take the dogs along. I'll show you how to trim the little hairs on their paws. Keeps ice balls from forming between their toes."

A while later, outside, we started across the lawn. The air was so cold the surface of the snow had crusted. I thought I heard footsteps behind me. I turned and saw it was the dogs. Papap walked beside me with a rifle. The sky was clear, a crystalline blue.

We crossed the tree line and entered the forest.

CHAIM POTOK was born and raised in New York City. He began to write fiction at the age of sixteen, graduated summa cum laude with a B.A. in English literature from Yeshiva University, and earned a Ph.D. in philosophy from the University of Pennsylvania. An ordained rabbi, he served as an army chaplain in Korea for sixteen months with, successively, a front-line medical battalion and an engineer combat battalion. His first novel, *The Chosen,* was nominated for a National Book Award and received the Edward Lewis Wallant Award. His other novels include *My Name Is Asher Lev, The Gift of Asher Lev* (winner of the National Jewish Book Award), and *I Am the Clay.*